Chapter 1

"Please be different? Please?" Samantha Felton, Sammy to everybody she knew, prayed the words aloud while standing in front of the bathroom mirror with her eyes closed tight. She took a deep breath in, held it a moment, released and slowly opened her eyes to stare at the woman in the mirror. With a sigh, she looked into the same chocolate brown eyes, that always seemed tired, looked at the same too round face. Ran her fingers through her boring reddish-brown hair. "Same old me," she said to herself, taking a step back to look at herself in the full-length mirror behind the door. Her faded blue jeans hugged her curves- all fuller than she wanted, and her t-shirt seemed to show off more of the unwanted weight she just couldn't seem to shake. With another aggravated sigh, Sammy brushed out her hair, braided it so it hung in a thick plat down her back and then left the bathroom.

"Being old sucks," she announced as she entered the small sunshine yellow kitchen, where her best friend and roommate, Lucy Kandler, stood at the stove cooking breakfast. Her raven black hair was pulled up in a messy bun, and she wore a pair of flannel pajama pants with pink flamingos on them and a hot pink tank top.

"You're thirty-four," Lucy said, plating up the eggs she had just finished. "Far from old." Her hazel eyes sparkled with laughter when she turned to face her friend.

"Easy for you to say," Sammy teased when Lucy placed a plate in front of her. "You're just a baby. Barely out of diapers." With a roll of her eyes and a click of her tongue, Lucy sat down opposite her.

"A baby? I'm only four months younger than you so if I'm a baby so are you. Now, no more talking about being old and let's say grace."

"All I'm saying," Sammy continued after a quick blessing, "is I'm not even close to what I thought I would be doing when I was this age, and for some reason aging isn't slowing down."

"You know there's only one alternative to growing old, right?" Lucy took a bite of her food before going on. "And you own your own shop *and* your own house." Lucy waved her fork in a circle to indicate the whole house. "Not to mention, you have the most wonderful best friend anyone could ever ask for. What more do you want?"

"The most wonderful, maybe, but not necessarily the most modest."

"Hey, just stating a fact. But seriously, what do you think you're missing?"

"Oh, I don't know, a Tesla would be nice. A beach house or two. Oh, I know…"

"A husband?" Lucy interrupted, with a smirk perched on her lips.

"No," Sammy quickly answered shaking her head hard. "Absolutely not. I gave up on that dream a long time ago. Who would want a boring thirty-something year old curvy book nerd?"

"Who wouldn't? And thirty-something isn't too old to get married, you know," Lucy pointed out. "A ton of people are waiting until their thirties to get married and start families. You make it sound like we're on death's door. You aren't an old maid. You're not becoming the neighborhood spinster. We may be growing old together but, sister, we ain't there yet."

"Anyhow," Sammy started as she got up to rinse off her plate. "I'm not asking for much, and I love what I do, but..." She left the sentence hanging, while she put her plate in the dishwasher and turned to look at her friend.

"But a little excitement wouldn't hurt?" Lucy threw out there. Sammy gave her a tight smile and nodded.

"Exactly. Life's a little too predictable nowadays. I get up, I go to work, I come home. Boring with a capital b."

"Well, as I'm who you currently come home to, I'm not sure how I feel about that statement."

"You know what I mean, Lucy. Isn't there supposed to be more to life? Adventure? Excitement? Something? When did life become so routine?" Lucy stood and put an arm around Sammy's shoulders.

"Well, if excitement won't come to us, let's go to the excitement. Let's do something wild and crazy this weekend. We can have a Sammy-Lucy Wild Girl Weekend."

"You mean like the Women's meeting on Saturday afternoon or the Over 30's Small Group on Sunday morning? Or are we going to go really crazy and- gasp, go into the Friendship Class on Sunday instead? We really would be babies in there."

"There's more to life than church," Lucy said. "Why don't we go out to dinner and a movie on Friday?" Sammy laughed and hugged her friend.

"Man, what am I going to do with you? You're going real cray-cray on me." Lucy laughed too and pushed her friend toward the front door.

"Go on," she said. "I'll keep thinking about this problem. Who knows? Maybe something will blow in on the wind."

"The only thing that ever blows in on the wind around here is a bad smell from the farms at the edge of town." Sammy laughed at the face Lucy made, before heading out of the kitchen.

Sammy walked the short three blocks from her house to Main Street and took in the morning activities. It wasn't quite Spring on the calendar yet, but the weather was already warm enough that she had left her jacket at home, and the flowers were starting to poke up through the ground. Taking a deep breath of crisp air, Sammy smiled at the bustling little street that ran through the center of downtown. Mrs. Castleberry was just opening the doors to her quirky little vintage upcycle jewelry store, *Love-Sparkle-Vintage,* when she noticed Sammy and waved. "Good morning, Sammy," she called. Sammy waved back and continued her way, preferring not to get caught up in one of Mrs. Castleberry's two-hour long conversations. Next to that store was a little antique shop, *Fleas n' Tiques*, owned by Devin Carter. He had been Sammy's history teacher in high school and loved everything dealing with the past. So, when he retired a few years back, it came as no surprise that he finally opened the store he always talked about. Across the street was an old-fashioned hardware store and the local pharmacy.

After a quick stop by the *Better with the Bean Coffee Shop* to see Martha Calloway and grab herself her favorite Monday morning pick me up- a Salted Carmel Latte and a cheese Danish, Sammy arrived at the front door of her own little piece of the American dream, *By the Book*. The cutest, coziest, and only bookshop in downtown or a 25-minute radius. Holding her coffee in one hand, she pulled her keys out of her bag and let herself in, flipping around the Open sign, before turning off the alarm. Sammy reached over and turned on the lights and smiled as the rows of books were illuminated in a bright glow. Just seeing all the books made her heart happy. She deposited her bag behind the counter, clicked on her computer, and then set about putting on a pot of coffee. It wasn't the best coffee around, but a lot of her customers liked to sit and enjoy a cup while starting their newest adventure. Not to mention, a hot pot of coffee convinced a lot of people to stay and chat, and often a chat would lead to Sammy recommending a new book which led to a sale.

Sammy had just finished stocking some new books when the door of the bookstore flew open, and a blonde hair girl walked in. "Good morning, Miss Sammy," she called out. "Mama is coming. She's getting Jude out of the car seat."

"Good morning, Suzanna," Sammy greeted the girl. She watched as Suzanna made her way to one of the leather chairs and plopped down in it. Her blonde hair was up in two pigtails and her blue eyes sparkled with mischief. Today she was wearing her favorite color- in the form of a pink shirt with a pink skirt, and big clunky rainbow colored rainboots. Sammy smiled at the combination. "Did you have a good weekend?" she asked the girl as she came around to join her.

"I sure did. We went hiking with Uncle Noah."

"Uncle Noah?" Sammy didn't remember her ever talking about having an uncle, let alone one in this town. Curiosity tugged at her.

"Yeah, he's in town for a bit. Mama said he's thinking about moving here. I hope he does cause he's really fun and smart and he gives us piggyback rides and sometimes he reads us books before bed."

"Oh, he does sound like fun," Sammy commented.

"And he promised that soon me and him would have a day out, just us."

"I see that Suzanna is filling you in on her Uncle Noah," Janet Miller said, as she came through the door with a large bag on her shoulder and three-year-old Jude by the hand. "Sorry she left the door open again," she said with a stern stare at her daughter. "We are working on that."

"Sorry, mama," Suzanna said with a shy grin. Janet couldn't stay mad long, and soon replaced her scowl with a bright smile.

"Expecting a lot of people at the book club today?" Sammy asked, sitting down next to Suzanna.

"About the normal," Janet replied. "I really

appreciate you letting us host a homeschool club here. It's so hard to find a place willing to let a bunch of homeschoolers take over for a few hours and honestly, we get tired of hosting things out of our homes and cleaning up the aftermath."

"No problem," Sammy said, as Jude climbed into her lap for a hug. "I think it's awesome that you homeschool these two rug rats and honestly, if I ever have kids, you've convinced me that homeschooling is the way I want to go."

"I know it's not for everybody, but we love it. It's a little different now that Noah is staying with us. Luckily, he's normally out of the house during the day, and well, we just play it by ear when he's not." Sammy tickled Jude and then looked up at his mom.

"So, Uncle Noah is your brother?" she asked. She had only known Janet a year or so but had only heard her talk about a sister.

"Yup, he's mine," Janet answered with a laugh. "My little brother, although he's taller than me now, so I guess I should really say he's my younger brother. Hey, you should meet him." Sammy knew that look and quickly shook her head.

"Oh no. Don't even think about it. I'm not interested in dating."

"I never mentioned dating," Janet said with a grin. Sammy opened her mouth to restate that she wasn't looking to date anybody, when the door opened and two more families for the homeschool book club walked it. Sammy gave a sigh of relief as she put Jude down and both kids followed the group into the back room. She was just about to stand when Janet popped her head out through the doorway. "Did I mention he sings and not half bad looking…you know, for a brother?" Janet disappeared with a giggle before Sammy could say anything else.

The bookstore was quiet, even for a Tuesday. After the excitement of Monday's book club, it was a bit of a letdown to have only two customers all day. Sammy had already rearranged books, dusted the pictures on the wall, answered seven emails, checked on the status of her latest Amazon purchase, and now she stood by the front window, redoing her display. With a sigh, she moved the same book she had just moved back to the place she had moved it from. Some days running a little bookstore was not the most fun a girl could have. Sammy was about to turn away from the window when a flash caught her eye. Coming to a stop across the street from her was an old truck the brightest shade of yellow she had ever seen. Like most people standing on the street, Sammy couldn't help but to stare at it- mouth open- in disbelief. Then she couldn't hold back anymore. She was grateful that no one else was in the store at that moment because she barked out a loud laugh. She quickly put a hand over her mouth, on the off chance that the person behind the wheel glanced at her way, and snickered until her eyes watered, no real idea why she found the yellow truck so amusing. Then the truck door opened, and Sammy craned her neck to try and catch a quick glimpse of the driver. Some old hippie geezer, no doubt. However, one last snicker got caught in her throat as the man inside stepped out.

He was tall with broad shoulders. His dark brown hair hung too long for Sammy's normal taste in men, however it seemed to fit him perfect. He was wearing jeans, a black button up shirt- untucked- cowboy boots and sunshades. The hand over her mouth wasn't there to conceal her laugher anymore, but to hide her slack jaw stare. "Oh my," she said to herself. She stood at the window and watched the man, who looked up and down the street, like he was looking for something, until a tap on her shoulder made her scream and whirl around. "Don't do that to me," she scolded, with her hand over her heart.

"You okay?" Lucy asked, concern in her hazel eyes and amusement on her face.

"I'm fine," Sammy snapped, pushing past her friend before she caught on to what she was staring at.

"And so is he," Lucy commented followed by a low whistle. Too late. Sammy walked behind the counter and grabbed her water bottle, her mouth suddenly dry.

"Who is?" she asked, trying to sound innocent before taking a long swig of water. Lucy continued to look out the window for a moment more, before turning around to face Sammy.

"You know who. That's why you didn't hear me come in. You were in ga-ga land over mister tall, dark, and handsome."

"Don't you think that saying is overdone?" Sammy questioned hoping to turn the conversation away from her.

"You got a little drool about there," Lucy teased pointing to the side of her own mouth. Sammy felt her face heat up and knew it was turning red, yet still she denied everything. The last thing she needed was Lucy causing a scene, and Sammy knew she would. If she knew one thing about her long-time friend, it was that she never turned down a chance to make a big scene.

"Don't be ridiculous," Sammy started, as she picked up a stack of papers and shuffled through them. "I was just thinking about the big street fair in a few months. I need to figure out how I'm going to draw people into the store." Lucy crossed her arms over her chest and looked at Sammy in disbelief. Sammy squirmed under her gaze, until she finally uncrossed her arms and walked over to the coffee maker and poured herself a cup. Sammy placed the papers back on the counter and tried to look anywhere but at her best friend.

"You know I don't believe you, right?" Lucy asked, as she sat down and crossed her legs. "But I'm going to let you off the hook. *This* time." Sammy glanced over at her friend and narrowed her eyes at the sly grin on Lucy's face. "Anyhow, I'll get my answer during the show."

"What show?" Sammy asked, suddenly suspicious and nervous. The grin on Lucy's face spread into a full-blown evil smile.

"Mr. Hotness is about to walk in." Just as she said it, the bell over the door chimed, and Sammy's world froze. She felt her stomach drop and her breath get caught. Lucy gave a wink and brought her cup to her lips.

"Excuse me." The voice behind her was deep, with a faint Southern drawl. Sammy licked her lips, shot her friend a death glared that she hoped read *I'm gonna kill you* and then turned around with a smile- or what she hoped was a smile- on her face.

"Yes, welcome to By the Book. How can I help you today?" *Does my voice really sound like that?* she thought to herself. Overly cheerful? Breathe. Just breathe. The man in front her, smiled back, seemingly unaware Sammy's nerves.

"I'm looking for a book," he said. "Well, I would be, huh? Being as this is a bookstore and all." He coughed to clear his throat and she noticed red creeping up from his collar. *Good,* she thought. *I'm not the only one nervous.* Although that thought made her even more uncomfortable.

"Good thing for you, the morning crowd has been slow today, so I have one or two books left of the shelves." Sammy felt herself slipping back into her normal self. Men she was clueless about. Books, however, were her love language. "What kind of book are you looking for? And don't say one with words." The man gave her a lopsided smile.

"For a baby," he said. "Well, really for the parents." The man reached up and rubbed the back of his neck. "Let's try this again. A friend of mine and his wife just had their first baby, and I would like to give them a book as a gift." His glance bounced around the store, skipping over Lucy sitting smugly in a leather chair and then settled back on Sammy. "So, I'm thinking maybe a murder mystery might be out of the question." He smiled again, and Sammy returned it. *A man with a sense of humor*, she thought. *Thank goodness.*

"Probably need to wait until at least the first birthday," she answered, coming around the counter. "The baby books are right this way, I'm sure I have just the thing." She led the way to the corner where she had all the kids' books, plus a few other gift items. Picking up a blue hardback book, she turned and handed it to him.

"This is one of my favorites," she told him. "The one I normally give as a gift. All about how much of a blessing a baby is and about how God sent the perfect little one to the parents. It's very sweet." Sammy waited as the man flipped through the book, stopping to read a page or two, and then nodded.

"I think this will be perfect," he said. "Thank you very much." After she had rung the man up and he had paid, she couldn't help but ask the question burning in her mind.

"So, what's with the banana truck?" She regretted the question when he gave a nervous laugh and the red started creeping back up his neck.

"Yeah, she's an attention getter, alright. Hard to miss."

"She?" Sammy arched one eyebrow up in question.

"The truck," he said, jabbing a thumb over his shoulder. "A 1977 Chevrolet C-10 Bonanza, to be precise." Sammy stared at him for a moment, and then felt the edges of her mouth twitch. "But I guess unless you are a truck person, that doesn't really mean much. I can tell you want to laugh. What's so funny?" Sammy bit her lip. "It's okay, I can take it."

"I'm sorry," she finally said. "I don't mean to laugh. *She's* a nice truck and all."

"I feel a *but* coming."

"But…," she half said half snorted. "You have a… jackpot of bananas. A *Banana Bonanza*." Lucy coughed in her coffee behind her and Sammy had to put a hand to her mouth to keep from laughing. The man stood there looking at her with mild interest for a moment, before he started laughing too.

"I guess," he started, "when you say it like that, it is pretty funny. I normally just say she's yellow and no, I have no idea why the previous owner painted her that color."

"Yellow," Sammy repeated, nodding her head. "Good idea, lets stick with yellow."

"I'm Noah, by the way" he said, holding out his hand. Sammy hesitated a moment before taking it.

"Sammy," she said, her mind racing to figure out where she had heard that name recently. "Noah? That wouldn't be as in *Uncle* Noah, would it?" Noah gave her a questioning stare. "I know Janet," she hurried to explain. "Suzanna was telling me you took her hiking. That was really sweet of you."

"Just trying to earn Uncle of the Year."

"Does she have any other uncles?" Sammy questioned, aware that she was being nosey.

"Nope," Noah answered with a shake of his head. "Should mean I'm a shoe in, but you can never tell with kids nowadays." He gave her another smile. "Well, I guess I need to be going. I hope to see you around." Sammy answered with a smile of her own and watched as he turned and walked away.

"Don't say it," Sammy threatened the moment the door closed after Noah. "Don't you dare say it."

"Not gonna say a word," Lucy answered, but Sammy could hear the smirk in her voice.

Chapter 2

Sammy looked forward to Wednesday. The bookstore always peaked up a bit on Wednesday for some reason and she had the Mid-Week service to look forward to as well. Starting at six in the evening, her church served a five-dollar dinner and then at seven the service began. It was always more upbeat than on Sunday. With fast music and Pastor Gene always gave a quick, to the point- often livelier sermon. Sammy smiled to herself as she approached the church and felt a calm wash over her just entering the parking lot. She knew some people didn't go to church, or at least didn't go Sunday and Wednesday, but she enjoyed the fellowship- and food- that came with being involved. It also recharged her batteries, made her feel like she could take on the world and the people who came into her store.

Sammy drove around the parking lot looking for Lucy's car when she spotted a bright Banana Bonanza. *He really seemed like a nice guy*, she thought to herself. *And good looking.* If Sammy knew anything, it was the nice, good-looking guys didn't date women like her. Women who were already in their thirties. Women who wore a size 14 instead of a size 4. Women who owned their own business and house. Women who rather stay home reading books or playing video games- yes, she played video games and loved it, then go out parting on the town. Women who had a servant's heart and was often busy volunteering at church or for some other non-profit. *Yup, they don't go for women like me.*

Pulling into a parking place a few spots down, she let her eyes drift over toward the truck, and saw Noah sitting behind the wheel, eyes closed, head tilted back on the back window. She knew she shouldn't stare but couldn't pass up the chance to take in his features, even if it was from afar. Suddenly, almost as if he sensed her gaze, he opened his eyes and turned his head toward her. Caught red handed, Sammy forced a smile and a small wave, then quickly dropped her eyes, and began playing with her phone. A tap on the window moments later made her jump.

"Sorry," Noah called through the closed window. Sammy turned off the engine, reached for her purse and opened the door. He took a step back to allow her room to get out. "I didn't mean to startle you," he said.

"That's ok. I was just asking Lucy where she was. Didn't see you get out your truck." She held up her phone to prove her point.

"Lucy?" he questioned.

"The, um, the other girl in the shop yesterday," Sammy clarified, wondering how somebody, especially a man, could forget about the beautiful bombshell. "She's my best friend and my current housemate until she finds a new place. The place she was renting got sold and well, that left her homeless. Of course, that was seven months ago. The market has been whacky." Sammy mentally kicked herself for rambling, something she often did when she was nervous.

"I know that feeling. Before coming here to stay with Janet, I shared a little apartment with a friend. Trying to find a place to rent was tough in the best of times, but now, it just seems like people have gone crazy." Sammy nodded and closed her car door.

"Are you meeting Janet here for dinner?" she asked, desperate for something to say, and refusing to talk about the weather.

"Yes," he replied. "I'm also here," but his sentence was cut short by the scream of a little girl.

"Uncle Noah!" Suzanna called running up to him with her arms up. Noah picked her up mid run and swung her around. "I'm so happy to see you," she said, hugging him tight around the neck. "It's been forever."

"It's been since about 2 o'clock," Janet said walking up to them, carrying Jude.

"Feels like forever," Suzanna stage whispered. Sammy laughed at the girl's affection toward her uncle. "Hi, Miss Sammy," she said, noticing her for the first time. "You know my Uncle Noah?" She asked, giving Noah another tight squeeze around the neck.

"I do indeed," Sammy answered, returning the girls smile. "He stopped by the bookstore yesterday, and you know that once you come into my store, you're a friend for life."

"Would you like to join us for dinner?" Janet asked, a note of pleasure in her voice. "Ken will be here in a few minutes," she explained of her husband. "He had to work a little late today." Sammy kept her eyes trained to Janet but could feel Noah watching her. Could feel heat raising up her neck.

"No, thank you," she declined. "I wouldn't want to intrude on family time. And anyhow," she pushed on before Janet could reply, "I'm meeting Lucy. She should be here soon."

"Well, you both are welcome to join us," Janet said. "Come on, you two, let's go get in line." Sammy let out a breath as she watched Janet, Noah, and the kids walk off.

Sammy and Lucy sat in the far corner of the fellowship hall. She was trying to pay attention to Lucy and her latest story, but her eyes kept drifting over to Noah, and she noticed so did the eyes of every other single woman in the place too. Without realizing it, she let out a deep sigh. "Am I boring you?" Lucy asked, stopping mid-sentence, and looking up at her friend. "I know I tend to go on and on, I'm sorry."

"No, I'm sorry," Sammy countered. "It's not you, I just have a lot on my mind."

"Like Mr. Hotness over there?" Lucy questioned with a smirk.

"Lucy, we are in a church, you can't call him that." What if Pastor Gene heard her? What if old Mrs. Tucker heard her? The good Lord knew that would lead to a strong lecture at the next Women's meeting.

"Please," Lucy said, rolling her eyes. "I might be a Christian, but I'm not blind. He's good looking. He's funny, from what I saw yesterday, and I would wager fifty dollars that he's single." Lucy said the last word in a sing song voice. "I may have checked out his hand for a ring while he was at the bookstore."

"And I'll wager fifty dollars that just about every

single female in here over the age of 18 is thinking the same thing. No," she said shaking her head. "I need to get him out of my mind and my mind on safer things. And yes, he's single. Janet has already tried to set us up and I told her the same thing I'm telling you; I'm not looking for a guy."

"If you say so," Lucy replied with a shrug. "But I don't see why you don't at least go talk to him."

"Well, for starters, he just left the room," Sammy teased. "Unless you're implying, I follow him."

"Now you're talking." Lucy rubbed her hands together.

"Lucy, there is no way, under the sun, on God's green earth that a man like that would ever be interested in me." Sammy was determined to make her friend see what she already knew. "Not that I want him to be."

"You keep saying that, but I just don't understand why? You're beautiful, and funny, and sweet and kind. What kind of guy *wouldn't* want to date you? You're quite the catch."

"Anyway," Sammy pushed on, "if you have forgotten, I'm not looking for a guy. I'm perfectly happy with my life." Before Lucy could speak, she continued. "Ok, maybe not perfectly happy, but I want to climb a mountain or go scuba diving or something like that. I am not looking for a man."

"Ok, ok," Lucy said, holding up her hands. "I get it. I heard you loud and clear. I just want you to be happy and if that means going scuba diving, then let's book a trip to Florida come summer." Sammy smiled. She really did have a good friend. "And, I mean, if you're not interested in him, maybe I'll just have to chat him up later." *Then again*, Sammy thought. *Maybe she's not that good of a friend.*

Sammy and Lucy sat in the sanctuary near the back, close to one of the exit doors. They had a meeting- hopefully a short one- right after service and being close to the door ensured that they wouldn't be late. As part of the Beautification Committee, it was their job to help keep the church decorated for the different holidays, and with spring officially just around the corner, it was time to change décor, weed the flower beds and generally make the church look warm, welcoming and fresh. The committee chair, Julie Cunningham, was good at what she did, and really nice, and she liked punctuality.

The chatter in the room started to die down as Pastor Gene Holt made his way on stage. He patiently waited for the last of the conversations to end, before greeting the congregation. "Good evening, everybody," he said, his voice deep and a little raspy from years of smoking before getting the call from the Lord to stop right before he was called to be a pastor. He was a tall gentleman with a lanky build. He didn't seem to have an ounce of fat on him, and often Sammy thought he looked somewhat uncomfortable with his height. His graying hair just barely touched the collar of his shirt, and he had the start of a 5 o'clock shadow on his face. Sammy loved listening to him talk about his life before becoming a pastor. He had been 41 years old, and according to him, hell of wheels. It gave her comfort knowing that God took this hellion who smoked and drank and turned his life around. Gave him a calling to be a preacher so that he could reach people for Him.

Sammy shook her head slightly to clear her thoughts when she realized that she had missed Pastor Gene's opening prayer. "I have a special treat for you today," he was saying now. "I know since June left a few months back, worship time on Wednesday and Sunday has been, well, a little less than stellar. Of no fault of our wonderful, piano player," he quickly added. "My old voice box just isn't cut out for singing anymore. So that's why I'm very pleased to announce that, although we haven't found a permeant replacement yet, we have managed to find a Worship Pastor in between churches at the moment and he has agreed to lead us for the next month or so." Pastor Gene waited for the murmuring to settle down again. "So, I would like to introduce to you all Pastor Noah Sinclair. Come on up, sir."

Sammy was halfway to clapping when she saw him stand. *Pastor Noah? Uncle Noah? Noah was a preacher!* Lucy must have heard the sharp intake Sammy did, because she looked over at her friend. "I'm going to hell," she whispered. "Talking about a pastor like that. I'm sure God doesn't look kindly on thinking a pastor is hot, well at least not saying it out loud." Sammy was too in shock to say anything back. She watched as Noah- no, *Pastor Noah* walked up on stage and shook Pastor Gene's hand. Then as the senior pastor left, Noah picked up the guitar that was sitting nearby and smiled out at everybody.

"Good evening," he said. "When my sister, Janet, told me the church was without a worship leader, little did I know that God would lead me here to help. But I'm glad he did." He began to warm up his guitar and fingers with some gentle strumming. "I've gotten to hang out with my niece and nephew, and I've met some really nice people in my short time in town." Lucy nudged Sammy's arm with her elbow, but Sammy only shook her head. "If you see a bright yellow truck," he said with a hint of laugher, "that's me and the Banana Bonanza, as one local resident has dubbed it." Lucy gave her another jab in the ribs.

"See? He's talking about *you*." Sammy was about to reply when Noah asked everybody who could stand to, and then started singing the first song of the night and it was beautiful. His voice was amazing. It touched her heart and lifted her spirit. And right then and there, Sammy was convinced life wasn't fair. Not one bit.

The meeting after service only lasted fifteen minutes, which Sammy was very thankful for. She stood around for a few minutes with Lucy and their friend, Carla, talking about plans they had for the weekend. After they all said goodbye, Lucy left so she could go by the store, leaving Sammy alone with her thoughts. Which sometimes was a very dangerous thing since she found them turning toward the good-looking Pastor Noah. The hallway was empty as she made her way to the front doors. Outside, the sun hung low in the sky, sending streaks of sorbet orange and cotton candy pink shooting out from the horizon. The outdoor lights illuminated the parking lot, and people stood around in small groups talking. Sammy had just come down the steps when one group of people caught her eye. Maryann and Jasmine had ganged up on Noah, who looked a bit like a frightened rabbit. Both women were extremely outgoing, fun loving and not shy about going after what they wanted. They had just started their own event planning company, specializing in bridal showers, baby showers and adult birthday parties, and their outgoing personalities made them good at what they did. Right now, however, it looked like they had their eyes set on reeling in Noah. *He looks so nervous,* she thought. *Is he supposed to be that shade of grayish green?* She had just turned away when something stopped her. Something in her heart felt sorry for him. With a deep breath, she turned back around and walked toward the small group. "Maryann! Jasmine!" she called out as she approached. "The baby shower last Saturday was amazing," she said, earning her smiles. "I'm so impressed by your talent."

"Sammy," Maryann cooed. "Thank you so much. We had such a fun time."

"That's right," Jasmine agreed. "And Lilly is such a sweet girl. I can't wait to meet the baby." Sammy smiled back. Maryann and Jasmine might be forces of nature, but they really were nice women who used their talents to help the community and to serve the Lord.

"And Pastor Noah," she continued. *Was he going to be sick?* "Just the person I was hoping to run into. The book that you ordered came in today." His eyes narrowed in confusion. "I have it in my car, if you would like to come get it?" She saw realization dawn in his eyes.

"Yes," he said, a little too enthusiastically, then quickly coughed to hide the slight crack in his voice. "That would be great. Thank you so much for bringing it." He looked at Maryann and Jasmine. "Ladies, if you'll excuse us." With that he gave them a smile, walked past, and motioned for Sammy to lead the way. "Thank you," he whispered when they were out of ear shot. His voice was laced with relief. "I'm not good with people."

"You were looking a little green around the gills back there," Sammy teased, trying not to laugh. "And if you aren't good with people, why on earth did you become a pastor? Which, I might add, came as a complete and total shock."

"Wait," Noah said as he stopped walking. "You didn't know?" Sammy continued the few paces to her car, unlocked it and opened the back door. She placed her purse inside and pulled out a small package.

"No, I'm afraid Suzanna didn't tell me that part about Uncle Noah," she answered, holding out a book. When Noah just looked at it, she explained. "You are still being watched. I said I had a book for you. Thus, here is a book."

"You just happen to carry books in your car to save men in distress?" he joked with a smile, as he reached out for it.

"I do own a bookstore," she answered closing the door and leaning her hip against it. "But this happens to be a personal book, so I would like it back."

"Of course."

"You never answered my question," she pointed out. "If you aren't comfortable with people, why become a pastor? Isn't that one of the requirements or something?" Noah rubbed the back of his neck. A nervous habit she's noticed.

"I'm comfortable with *people* people," he said.

"But you just said," Sammy started.

"It's *women* people," he interrupted, holding up a hand. "I mean, women who...you know, who flirt unabashedly." Sammy couldn't help the laugh that escaped her, and she quickly put a hand over her mouth to try and smother it. "Glad my discomfort gives you pleasure."

"I'm sorry, but you are about ten different shades of red right now. Look, Maryann and Jasmine may come across as..."

"Wolves in sheep clothing?" Noah offered.

"I was going to say a little overwhelming, but they really are nice women."

"Oh, no doubt," he answered. "Since they both invited me to lunch on Sunday." Sammy pushed away from her car, suddenly very aware that they stood in an almost empty parking lot. Maryann and Jasmine stood talking by their cars, occasionally glancing their way. Pastor Gene stood near the church talking to someone as his wife waited nearby. The last thing she needed was a rumor about her and the new pastor- *no, temporary Worship Leader*- going around.

"I should be going," she said, reaching for her door handle. "You can drop the book off at the store next time you're in town."

"Will do. And Sammy, thanks." He smiled again, and she hurried to get into her car and shut the door. *He's a pastor*, she thought to herself. *No thinking he's got a sweet smile.*

Chapter 3

Friday dawned bright and sunny, and Sammy wished she was anywhere else, but stuck in her bookstore. Which was so unlike her. Normally her store was her haven, her happy place. The place where she felt most at peace- next to church, at least. *Normally I'm not here every day, all day*, she thought. She had one part-time employee that came in serval times a week to give her a break, a chance to catch her breath and run errands, but Kathy was on a much-deserved vacation. Leaving Sammy in the store every day from open to closed. Now she sat on the floor in the children's section, straightening up books from a group of toddlers earlier that morning. The bell over the door dinged. "Welcome to By the Book," she called out. "I'll be with you in a moment." She finished stacking the last of the books and then pushed herself up off the floor. Happy with her work she turned around and screamed. "Don't do that," she said, putting a hand over her heart. "You scared me to death." Noah, who had moved to where she was on silent feet, just offered her a lopsided grin, although his eyes flickered with humor.

"Sorry," he said, holding out a cup from the coffee shop down the street. "I brought you a cup of coffee as a gift, but I guess now it's more like a peace offering."

"You brought me...coffee?" Sammy looked at the cup in his hand and then back to him. "Why?"

"Like I said, as a gift. A thank you," he said, suddenly wondering if this had been a good idea. "For saving me Wednesday night. I also brought back the book. It's on the front counter." Sammy took the cup and then pushed past him heading toward the front of the store where it wasn't as crowded with bookcases and items, or isolated. *Chicken,* a voice in her head mocked.

"Thank you," she said over her shoulder. "That was really nice of you." He followed her up and sat down in one of the chairs.

"I was at the church getting ready for Sunday, when all the music kind of started swimming together, so I thought it was time for a break and the perfect time to drop by. The lady down at the coffee shop said that was your favorite, so I hope she was right."

"You talked to Martha? About me?" she questioned. She looked down at the cup once more and then took a hesitant sip.

"Well, I didn't know what to get you and umm, it seemed like the sensible thing to do." Noah reached up and rubbed the back of his neck. This whole thing was not going the way he had envisioned it.

"You always rub the back of your neck when you're nervous," Sammy pointed out, matter-of-factly. "And yes, this is my favorite. Salted Carmel anything is my favorite." Noah dropped his hand from his neck. "So, do you have the music mostly ready to go then?"

"Mostly," Noah said with a nod. "Pastor Gene said he wanted four songs. I have them picked out, but I like to run through them a few times each before service. Pick out what I'm going to play." Sammy leaned against the counter and crossed her ankles.

"I thought you said you already had them picked out." she asked.

"Play as in which instrument," he clarified.

"You play more than one?"

"A few, but mostly I stick to the guitar. Easier to carry around." Sammy watched as he raised his cup and took a sip. "So why a bookstore?" he asked, looking around. "What makes someone wake up one day and decide to open a bookstore?"

"I like books," she answered with a one shoulder shrug. "Seemed like a good thing to do. Own a bookstore and I could spend my time reading. Come to find out, running a bookshop doesn't actually give me much time to read, at least not on most days. Guess I should have researched that more. What about you? Why a pastor and not a famous singer or something? With that voice of yours, I bet you could have made it big."

"Seemed like a more worthwhile adventure," Noah replied. Sammy studied him for a moment. She could tell there was more to the story than what he was saying. "I mean, I was in a band when I was younger, all through high school and into college." Sammy wasn't surprised by that. "But the more I sung, I don't know, the more things went wrong."

"Well, that sounds ominous." The bell over the door rang to indicate a customer.

"Welcome to By the Book," she said before turning around, sad that she had to take her attention away from Noah. "Oh, good morning, Maryann." She heard a quiet struggling noise from behind her, as Noah choked on his coffee.

"Good morning, Sammy and good morning, Pastor Noah," she purred as she walked around the counter. "Fancy meeting you here."

"Yes, hello Maryann," he said, as he stood. "I was just on my way out. Promised Janet I would watch the kids while she ran some errands." He gave Maryann a curt nod. "Sammy, thanks again. I'll talk to you later." And with that, he was out the door and headed down the street.

"He's an odd fellow," Maryann said, after they had both watched his retreating back.

"Maryann, I couldn't agree more." Turning her eyes to the other woman, she smiled. "What can I do for you today?"

Sammy rolled over in bed and stretched. It felt good to sleep in and know she didn't have anywhere to be. Kathy was back from vacation and was working all day. Leaving Sammy with a whole Saturday to just do whatever. And she loved that idea. The smell of bacon assaulted her nose and her stomach let out a loud growl. Lucy knew how to get her up and moving. She threw back the covers and reached for her housecoat. A quick stop by the bathroom, and she padded barefoot down the stairs. "Lucy, you're killing me," she said as way of greeting, as she walked into the kitchen.

"I know," Lucy answered. "But you don't need to sleep away the whole day."

"And just why not?" Sammy asked, pouring herself

a cup of coffee. "No work. Nothing at church. Just a whole Saturday of complete laziness." With a happy sigh she sat down at the table and blew across her coffee cup. "What is it?" she finally asked when Lucy stuck out her bottom lip in a pout.

"I was hoping you'll want to do a little shopping with me," she answered as she took a seat across the table. "I've got that wedding coming up for my cousin and well, I've been putting off buying something to wear."

"Lucy," Sammy said, shocked. "The wedding is in *two* weeks."

"I know, I know. I have plenty of time." Lucy ate a bite of eggs. "At least, if you'll help me shop." She gave her friend a bright smile. "That's what best friends do, right?" Sammy screwed her mouth up trying to look mad, but in the end, she met Lucy's smile and laughed.

"Yeah, I guess it is."

"Yay!" Lucy clapped her hands together in excitement. "Maybe you'll even find a few new outfits. Maybe something cute to wear to church tomorrow."

"And why would I want something cute?" Sammy questioned; one eyebrow raised.

"I don't know. Maybe to impress a certain pastor." Lucy laughed when Sammy threw a piece of bacon at her.

"I most certainly am not trying to impress anyone, especially Pastor Noah." Sammy shoveled food into her mouth, hoping that Lucy would get the hint and drop the conversation.

"I don't know why not."

"Should I count the reasons?" Sammy asked around

a bite of egg. "Starting with, I'm not looking for a guy." She took the last bite of eggs. She stood and crossed the kitchen and placed her plate in the sink.

"All I know is that if a handsome *single* guy was making eyes at me, I would be all over that."

"Then you wear a cute outfit to church."

"I always wear cute outfits to church," Lucy countered. "But I have a feeling that any special effort by me would be wasted on the good Pastor."

"I'm going to get dressed," Sammy said, turning and heading out of the kitchen.

"I'm just saying, stacking the deck in your favor couldn't hurt," Lucy called after her, only to be answered by the slamming of a door.

"That one looks great," Sammy said, with a nod but not much enthusiasm. They had been shopping all morning. Now it was past noon, and she was getting hangry for sure. "That color really goes with your skin." Lucy twisted and turned as she looked at herself in the mirror. The dress in question was a sleeveless emerald green dress that stopped at her knees. It had just a little sparkly to the material and flared out at her waist. "I mean, one could say you look gorgeous, but one wouldn't want that to go to your head." Lucy stuck out her tongue, and then went back to looking at herself.

"I don't know. You don't think it's too much?"

"Are you kidding? It looks great. Dressy enough for a wedding but easy enough to dress down for a date out on the town." At that, Lucy smiled. She ran her hands down the soft fabric and turned around to see the reflection of the back of the dress.

"Well, maybe."

"Look, tell you what," Sammy began. "You keep looking at yourself in the mirror and I'll walk down to the café and go ahead and order us some lunch. Greek salad or a turkey sandwich?" she asked, already gathering her stuff, and standing.

"I guess I have kept you all morning, haven't I?" She looked at herself in the mirror again. "Ok. I'm going to get it. I'll change, pay for the dress, and meet you down there. A turkey sandwich and soup please."

Sammy was happy to be out of the dress shop. It wasn't that she didn't enjoy shopping, but there were only so many dresses she could look at, and only so many places in this town to buy one. As she pushed the door open to the Little Café, she took a deep breath and her stomach growled. Luckily, there wasn't a line, and she quickly placed her order and found a small corner table. She was scrolling through Facebook when a cough interrupted her thoughts. Looking up, she expected to see the waitress with her food, but instead found Noah standing next to the empty chair, hands in the pockets of his jeans and a smile. "Good afternoon," he said politely. "I was just leaving when I saw you and thought I would say hello."

"Good afternoon," Sammy replied, setting her phone off to the side. "You're welcome to sit until Lucy gets here."

"So, what are you up to today?" he questioned, as he pulled out the chair and sat. "I thought you lived at the bookshop."

"Normally I do, but Kathy is back and is working today to give me a bit of a break. So, Lucy and I are out shopping, well, Lucy is shopping and I'm starving." Her stomach growled again, as if on cue, and Sammy could feel her face start to heat up.

"I have heard that shopping can work up quite the appetite," Noah agreed with a smile.

"How about you?" she quickly asked, changing the subject away from her and her noisy stomach.

"I had a working lunch with Pastor Gene," he said, as he leaned forward and folded his arms on the tabletop. "And now I'm off to do a little shopping myself, before meeting up with Janet and her crew for a game of disk golf down at the park."

"You play disk golf?" Sammy asked.

"No," he answered, "but I figured neither do they, so I stand a fairly good chance of winning." Sammy laughed at his logic.

"You must tell me how it goes," she said.

"I'm sure it'll be a story worthy of a sermon," he said with a mischievous grin, and Sammy suddenly realized where Suzanna got hers from.

"You know, you never did really answer my question from yesterday," Sammy told him, mirroring his position.

"And what question is that?"

"What made you decide to be a pastor? Other than it seemed like a worthwhile occupation."

"Well," he began slowly, his blue eyes darkened

with emotions. "That's a bit of a complicated story."

"I swear," Lucy interrupted, coming to a stop next to the table, "that cashier was slower than a sloth. Hi, Pastor Noah. Are you joining us for lunch?"

"Good afternoon, Lucy," he answered as he stood from the chair. "And no, I'll leave you ladies to eat, and I'll see you both in the morning." He gave them both a smile, a nod goodbye and then he turned and left the Little Café.

"So," Lucy began, as she dropped her bags to the floor, and smiled over at Sammy. "Just chattin' with the new Pastor, huh?"

"Temporary Worship Leader," Sammy corrected. "Heavy on the *temporary* and he was here with Pastor Gene. He just came over to be polite."

"See," Lucy said with a smirk, "I don't think he came over to *just be polite*. I have the feeling that if it was me sitting at this table, he might have waved, but he would have kept on going." Sammy squirmed in her seat, thankful that their food arrived before any more questioning, at least for now.

The air on Sunday morning held that special Spring scent and just felt like the world was ready to wake up and burst alive with color. Sammy smiled to herself as she took a deep breath of it. She loved Spring. Of course, she also loved Autumn, and Winter really wasn't that bad either. Oh, and don't forget Summer. Ok, maybe Sammy just loved what each season had to offer. "Don't you love Spring?" she asked aloud, glancing over at Lucy who was getting out of the passenger side of her car.

"Absolutely," Lucy agreed. "The season of birth, and

color and picnics and love." Lucy held out love for about six seconds, batting her eyelashes and looking all goo-goo eyed at Sammy, who just laughed.

"The only one looking for love, my friend, is you." They fell into step beside each other as they started across the parking lot. Sammy quickly spotted the Banana Bonanza and averted her eyes back to the church.

"Mm-hmm," Lucy teased. "I noticed you're wearing that sundress that just happens to show off all the right curves without showing off all the wrong places." Lucy tried not to laugh as Sammy smoothed a hand down over it.

"What?" she questioned. "A girl can wear a dress to church. And it's a lovely day, and we *are* going out to lunch afterwards, right?"

"Mm-hmm," Lucy hummed again and this time she didn't bother to hide her giggle. "And I noticed that you put a little extra effort in doing your hair." Sammy gave a huff, which only made her friend laugh more.

"Just trying to focus on self-care," Sammy defended. "All the experts say it's super important."

"Whatever you say, Samantha Dear," Lucy laughed as they entered the front doors of the church. "I've got to find Ms. Julie before church. Toodles." And with a wiggle of her fingers, she was gone down the hall.

"May I call you Samantha?" Sammy's world stood still, and a shiver ran down her spine at the sound of her name rolling off Noah's lips in a low, deep voice. Turning, she found him dressed in black slacks and a black sports jacket over a pale blue shirt. His mouth tugged up on one side in a crooked smile. It took Sammy a moment to find her composure.

"Pastor Noah, how nice to see you," she said, instead of answering his question.

"Always a pleasure," he replied, with a slight dip of his head. "I'm afraid the disk golf didn't go as I had planned, and Suzanna won the whole thing. Milkshake prize and all."

"Good for her," Sammy laughed. "I must remember to tell her congrats."

"Oh, please don't," Noah said, holding up a hand. "That'll just lead to a lot of bragging on her part and how her uncle might have ended up with a disk in a tree." He shook his head. "And I'm afraid my tree climbing skills aren't what they used to be. It was all very sad."

"Now I must ask her," she said with another laugh.

"Pastor Noah," Pastor Gene called out from the doorway of his office. "May I steal you away from Miss. Sammy for a moment." And then to Sammy he apologized. "I am sorry, Sammy, I wouldn't interrupt if it wasn't important."

"Of course, Pastor," Sammy smiled. "I'll talk with you later, Pastor Noah." Noah watched her walk away for a moment before turning and following Pastor Gene into his office.

"How may I help you?" Noah asked, as Gene motioned for him to take a seat, after closing the door.

"Well, I called you in to talk about an…opportunity, but I must say," the older man got a twinkle in his eyes. "You seem to be quite smitten with our lovely Miss. Sammy."

"Just a friend," Noah replied, even though he wasn't so sure if friendship was all he was looking for. He found himself coming up with excuses to go into town with the hope of seeing her. At night, while he tried to read, his thoughts kept turning back to Sammy and their conversations.

"Time will tell us that," Gene said, with a knowing smile. "Noah," he said, more serious this time. "The church board has officially opened up the position for a new worship leader, a worship *pastor*. I know that you have agreed to be here for a month or so, for which we are extremely grateful, but I'm asking, would you consider putting your name into the hat?" Gene slid a folder across the table. "All the information is in there." Noah looked at the folder, afraid to actually touch it. "I'm not asking for an answer right now, but please, would you pray about it? See where God is leading you?" Noah swallowed hard but nodded his head as he picked up the folder. "Good, good," Gene said with a smile. "There's no rush," he continued. "Just take your time, and in the meantime, getting to know Miss Sammy a little better couldn't hurt."

"I'm not looking for a relationship," Noah quickly said.

"Noah, my boy, very few of us find love when we are actually looking for it."

Chapter 4

Noah had a hard time focusing. Not only was the conversation with Pastor Gene in the forefront of his mind, but when he came into the sanctuary before service began, he saw Sammy laughing with a man he hadn't met yet. They had seemed to be enjoying themselves, and Noah felt fire begin to burn in his belly when she reached out and touched the other guy's arm. *No room for jealousy*, he told himself. *Plus, what right do I have?* He found his spot on the front pew, closed his eyes, and prayed. A jealous pastor was not a good combination. By the time Pastor Gene said prayer and called him up to sing, the fire had died down, but he still felt uneasy about the whole thing. However, once he started strumming the guitar and everybody joined him in singing, he let the music flood his soul. This was always where he felt the closest to God- immersed in His music. Lifting his voice in praise. Letting his heart be free to feel, without thought, without worldly influence.

Once finished, Noah replaced his guitar and walked down to his seat. Thoughts of Sammy being pushed aside so that his whole focus was on Pastor Gene. The older man, stood and walked slowly up the steps, in no hurry to break the spell of the songs, of the praise. Even once he made it to the pulpit, he didn't speak. The room was deafly quiet as they watch their Pastor close his eyes in a personal prayer. "Sometimes," he finally said. "Sometimes we are faced with decisions that we don't feel equipped to make. We have choices in front of us, that we just aren't capable of making." Again, he paused and let his eyes move across the faces staring back at him. "It's in those times, the times of tough decision making that we find ourselves with an even bigger choice to make. Do we follow God and trust him to lead us, or do we follow ourselves, in our human need for control, too afraid to let go?" Noah felt the words in his soul. Pastor Gene seemed to be talking directly to him. His eyes drift closed once again, and he let the sermon wash over him. *Control*, he thought. That was something he knew a thing or two about. *Lord*, he began to pray, *help me*. That seemed to be as far as he could go. The words to continue escaped him, but he knew God knew his heart, even when Noah didn't know himself.

The sermon came to an end. Pastor Gene offered an ending prayer and people, all in a trace from the powerful words, began to stand and make their way out of the church. Pastor Gene stood by the main door to shake hands and offer a word of encouragement as people filed out. "Good Sermon, Pastor," Noah said when it was his time. "Very timely."

"God has a way of giving us what we need to hear when we need to hear it." The two men shook hands. "I'm here to talk whenever you're ready." Noah's lips pressed into a thin line. He gave a quick nod before he headed out of the doors into the Spring sunshine. It took a moment for his eyes to adjust and track down Sammy, standing with the man from before church. That burn flared in the bottom of his belly again as he made his way down the front steps. As much as he wanted to speak to her again, he was determined not to interrupt her conversation. Not to intrude on her life. However, he couldn't keep his eyes from drifting over to her again.

"Wonderful song choices," Maryann said, coming up to him, smiling. Noah forced his eyes away from Sammy and onto Maryann. She wore a pink sleeveless dress, with white roses on it. Her strawberry blonde hair hung loose around her face and her brown eyes sparkled in the sunshine. Her lips matched the pink of her dress perfectly, and the light scent of her perfume floated on the air. For the first time, Noah realized that she was a beautiful woman, and on top of her looks, she was talented and active in the church. A woman that any man would love to go out with, but he also realized that he felt no attraction toward her.

"Thank you," Noah answered. He forced his gaze not to seek out Sammy, wondering if she would save him again. And then mentally kicking himself for his own insecurities. "God seems to have a way of leading me to the right music."

"Absolutely. I can tell that you enjoy what you do, and your voice is absolutely enchanting." Maryann tucked a piece of hair behind her ear. "Pastor, I was wondering. Would you like to join us for Sunday dinner? Us being Jasmine and my parents and brother. We would love to have you." She batted her long eyelashes at him.

"Ah, yes, well, you see, Maryann," he started, his words stumbling over each other. He realized that he didn't have a good reason to turn her down.

"Ready to go, Noah?" Pastor Gene asked, coming

up behind him and placing a hand on his shoulder. "I promised Esther that we wouldn't be too late for lunch." Noah shot him a quick look and then nodded, suddenly thankful for all the years in drama club.

"Of course, Pastor," he said and then turned back to Maryann. "I'm sorry, Maryann, thank you for the invitation, but I already have plans." He stopped short of saying maybe next week, knowing full well, that she would take him up on that offer. For half a second, he felt bad because she really did seem disappointed, but just as fast she brightened up again.

"Oh, I understand," she said. "I wouldn't miss Ms. Esther's cooking either. Maybe another time." With that she smiled at them both, giving Noah a little more attention, and walked away.

"You're looking a little green there, my boy," Gene said with a laugh, as he patted Noah on the back. "Esther has already left, so I do need a ride home, if you don't mind. And we really would love to have you stay. Can't have Maryann finding out otherwise." Noah swallowed hard as he led the way to his Bonanza.

"I promise I'm not leading her on or anything," Noah clarified as they got into his truck.

"Of course not," Gene agreed. "I've never known Maryann to need leading." The older man laughed. "Maryann is a sweet girl, and incredibly talented, and she's going to make a wonderful wife one day, I'm sure, but I don't see you two as a good match." Holding up a hand he quickly continued, "I mean, if you were looking for a relationship, which I think I remember you saying you weren't."

"I've got too much stuff going on," Noah said, trying to convince himself more than Gene. "I come with too much baggage. Plus, I'm only here for a month." With that, Noah cast one last look over to where Sammy and mystery guy stood talking, and then pulled out of the parking spot.

"Brock Londoe." Gene said, as if reading his mind.

"What?" Noah kept his eyes looking out the front windshield.

"The guy talking to Sammy. His name is Brock Londoe. Him and Sammy dated for a time in high school." Gene chuckled when Noah gave him a questioning look. "I've been at this church a very long time," he said. "All these young people grew up with my kids. I know more about them than they think. Anyhow, Brock moved away after school, first off to college and then the Army. He's recently out of the military and back visiting his parents for a few weeks."

"Good to know," Noah muttered, tightening his grip on the steering wheel. Gene didn't say anything else, but Noah swore he saw the old man smile before he turned away to look out his window.

Sammy whistled to herself Tuesday morning as she opened a box of new books to put on the shelves. New books always put her in a good mood. She loved the way the smell tickled her nose. The way the covers felt under her hand. Each new book was a chance to explore a new place. A chance to lose yourself. The bell above the door dinged pulling her back to the reality of the bookstore. "It's just me, Samantha." That same shiver from Sunday went down her spine, and she couldn't help the smile that tugged at her lips as she turned around and saw Noah standing by the front counter. Today he was the most casual she had seen him, in jeans and a t-shirt that read *But first, Praise.*

"Good morning, Pastor," she said, putting the last book on the shelf, picking up the box, and making her way up front towards him.

"Please, it's just Noah," he corrected, as he moved to the coffee maker and got a cup before taking a sit.

"I thought it was disrespectful to drop the title," Sammy said, half teasing, as she put the box behind the counter.

"Not when the person in question has asked you to. How are you today?" Sammy followed suit and got herself a cup of coffee before perching on the front edge of one of the other chairs.

"I'm very well," she answered. "Are there times that I should call you Pastor? I'm curious." She took a sip of coffee while she waited, interested to hear his answer.

"Well, around children. We should always try to teach respect. And in business settings, like a church committee meeting or something, I guess."

"And when seeking advice from you in your official capacity?" Sammy tossed out. Noah choked on his coffee but quickly recovered, lowering his cup.

"Yes, I suppose then too." He leaned forward, arms resting on his knees. "Do you…do you need advice from me in my official capacity?" he questioned; his voice laced with worry.

Sammy took another slow sip of her coffee and

watched him over the rim of her cup. His face wasn't red, but he did look uncomfortable.

"No," she finally answered. The corners of her mouth twitched as she tried not to smile. "Not right at the moment. Oh, don't look so relived," she laughed.

"I wanted to talk to you after church on Sunday," Noah began, changing the subject. He sat back in his seat. "But I'm afraid Maryann tracked me down and then Pastor Gene and I needed to get moving to his house before Ms. Esther had both our hides."

"She would too," Sammy agreed. "She doesn't like lunch to be kept waiting. Why did you want to talk to me?" She cocked her head to one side and waited.

"Why?" When Noah brought up Sunday, he was hoping to get some information about Brock Londoe- like did they go out to lunch? Are they dating again? Is he back in her life? All questions he knew he didn't have a right to wonder about, let alone ask aloud. But he was still hoping for answers and instead he got a *why*. "Ah, well," his hand started to go to the back of his neck, but he stopped himself and let it drop back to his lap. "You see, Suzanna has a T-ball game Thursday night, and I was wondering if you would like to go watch her? With me? And Janet and Ken, of course," he quickly added. Hoping she didn't think it sounded too much like a date. She watched him for a moment as she thought.

"T-ball?" *It wasn't really a date*, she told herself. And she would like to see Suzanna play. The girl had invited her to a game before. *Would people get the wrong idea? And why do I care?* "What time?" she finally asked.

"Seven o'clock. Down at the ball fields, but I guess

you probably knew that, huh?"

"Ok," she answered after what seemed like hours. "I'd love to watch Suzanna play. I work until six-thirty Thursday night, so I'll just meet you all down at the fields, if that's ok?"

"Absolutely," he quickly agreed. Just then the bell dinged, and Noah's heart sunk to see Brock sauntered in, dressed in baggy cargo shorts and a t-shirt with *Army* written across the front.

"Sammy," he said in a loud voice. "Just making sure we were still on for tonight. Oh, I'm sorry, I didn't know you had a costumer." Sammy shot Noah a look, before averting her eyes and standing up.

"Brock, what a lovely surprise," she said. "This is a friend of mine, Pastor Noah Sinclair. You remember, he led worship Sunday morning."

"Yeah, yeah, I remember. Nice to meet you, Pastor." Noah stood to shake his hand.

"Noah, this is Brock Londoe, he's a childhood friend who's in town visiting his parents."

"I think we were a little more than just friends," Brock threw in with a wink. "I mean, after all I was your first."

"Thanks for the coffee, Sammy," Noah said, interrupting before he heard just what exactly Brock was talking about- although he did have a few guesses. "I need to be going, I have a lunch meeting." He tossed his now empty cup in the trash. "It was nice meeting you, Brock. Bye, Sammy." With that he nodded to them both and then left.

"Nice guy," he heard Brock saying as the door closed behind him. "For a *pastor*." Sammy found herself a little disappointed that Noah didn't use her full name, embarrassed at what Brock had implied and sorry to see Noah go all at once.

"Aren't pastors supposed to be nice?" Sammy questioned, throwing her empty cup away. "I mean, I guess there are mean ones out there, but they aren't very good at their job then, are they?"

"True," Brock said, leaning in for a kiss, but Sammy ducked away. "Not to that stage yet, huh?" Sammy shot him a warning look and he held up his hands in defeat. "Ok, ok," he said. "Anyhow, I did stop by to make sure we were still on for tonight?"

"Yes," Sammy answered. "I'm looking forward to getting to know you again."

"I'm the same old Brock," he said, leaning on the counter, arms crossed. "I'll pick you up at seven," he said. "Be beautiful for me." Sammy worried her bottom lip as he gave her a wink, and then left the shop.

Maybe, she thought. *This wasn't a good idea.*

Chapter 5

"This a so not a good idea," Lucy said, as she sat on Sammy's bed watching her friend get dressed. She ran her hand up and down a soft, furry pillow, her eyes trained on Sammy.

"It'll be fine," Sammy reassured her. "It's just dinner with an old friend."

"Umm, I'm not sure if that's how Brock sees it," she said. "And what about Noah?"

"What about Noah?" Sammy looked at herself in the full-length mirror. "Do I look ok without looking…I don't know…" She ran her hands down the front of her shirt, and then turned to look at her side profile.

"Disparate?" Lucy offered. Sammy stuck out her tongue. "And don't play dumb with me. You have a hot dude following you around and you're going out with *Brock*." The way Lucy said his name made Sammy laugh.

"First of all, he's not some new strand of Covid, so you don't need to say his name like that," Sammy countered. "Secondly, Brock isn't bad looking, and thirdly, Noah is a *pastor,* not a *hot dude.* Plus, he's not following me around."

"Being a pastor does not affect your hotness," Lucy defended. "Noah is fifty times better looking than Brock-

and no, you can't deny that. *And* have you seen the way he looks at you? You don't think it's odd he gets nervous around every female under the age of 50 but you? Do you not think it's odd that he comes into your store but has only bought that one book? He sent you a shout out the very first night he led worship with that whole banana Bonanza statement. Girlfriend, he brought you coffee. Correction, he brought you your *favorite* coffee."

"Alright, that's enough," Sammy said. "Anyhow, I thought you said God didn't like you thinking about pastors as hot?" she teased, catching Lucy's eyes in the mirror.

"I was wrong," Lucy justified, raising her chin. "He's perfectly okay with finding a pastor attractive, which Noah is, and again, I ask, why are you going out with Brock?"

"Because I loved him," Sammy answered seriously, as she turned around and walked to the bed and sat down. "For all his faults, Lucy, Brock was my first love. I thought I had let that go a long time ago but seeing him again." Sammy shook her head. "Suddenly, all the *what ifs* came back. What if he hadn't left? What if I had gone with him? What if we had gotten married?" Lucy reached out and took Sammy's hand.

"We all have a first love, Sammy. Brock had his chance with you, and he blew it. He left town without a backwards glance."

"I know, but I can't help thinking about those what ifs." Sammy took a deep breath and stood. "Anyhow, how do I look?" Sammy wore faded jeans and a dress shirt the color of a ruby. It was nice looking, without being too dressy. Black sandals with sparkly rhinestones adored her feet, her hair was pulled back at the base of her neck and a short strand of black pearls hang around her neck. Lucy nodded her approval.

"You look amazing," she said. Sammy looked in the mirror one more time. She patted her gut and then turned to see her backside.

"I don't look, well, fat?"

"Girl!" Lucy said, throwing the furry pillow at her. "You look amazing. And you have two guys chasing you, I don't know why you think you are fat."

"Old habits, I guess." Sammy took a deep breath when the doorbell rang. "Wish me luck."

"Have a good time, Sammy. Just remember to stay true to yourself. And don't make a decision about Brock or Noah without really praying about it." Sammy nodded, picked up her purse and then headed downstairs.

"I hope this place is okay," Brock said, as they pulled into the parking lot of a local steak place. "I've been craving a good steak and, if I remember correctly, they have the best around. Or at least they use to."

"They still do," Sammy agreed as Brock pulled his car into a parking place and smiled over at her. She took in his brown eyes and chiseled chin. His short-cropped hair and the scar on his right cheek that he got playing football in middle school. He was handsome, no doubt, but for some reason she couldn't shake Noah's blue eyes or lopsided grin from her head.

"I'm really glad you agreed to come out with me tonight," Brock said, before getting out and coming around to open her door.

"Only as friends," she reminded him. She didn't want people to get the wrong idea about her, especially Brock. They were out as friends, just like she was meeting up with Noah on Thursday, simply as friends.

"I'm hoping to change your mind," he told her with a grin. He offered his arm, and they walked together across the parking lot and into the small restaurant. The lobby was warm and inviting. With green plants and comfortable-looking leather chairs. The hostess quickly found Brock's name on the reservation list and led them to a small table in the back of the dining room. The lights were down low, and the hostess quickly lit a candle on the table.

"Your waiter will be with you in a moment," the young girl said as Brock held out the chair for Sammy and then took his own. She placed menus in front of them both and then handed Brock a wine menu. She smiled at them both and hurried away.

"Should we have some wine?" Brock asked, picking up the menu and glancing over the choices.

"I don't mind if you do, but I don't drink anymore," Sammy informed him, taking the food menu, and opening it up.

"You don't?" he asked, a little shocked.

"Nope. For a few years in my twenties, I hit the bottle a little too hard. It really took over my life, affected my friendships and job. My whole life. There was a bad incident around 25 and I just decided that I didn't need that in my life anymore." Brock looked at the menu once again, as if deciding what he should do, but finally closed it and laid it to the side.

"We'll skip the alcohol tonight." He offered her a smile while picking up the food menu. "What do you feel like having tonight?" Sammy looked over her menu.

"Umm, I think maybe the steak and shrimp. I haven't had that in such a long time."

"That does sound good, but I think I'll just go with a big ole steak and potato." He looked up at her and then his eye drifted past her. "Isn't that Pastor Noah?" he asked. Sammy turned to glance over her shoulder. Noah was standing just at the doorway waiting for the hostess. He was dressed in black jeans and a sky-blue polo shirt. Sammy reminded herself not to stare but couldn't tear his eyes away until Brock started talking again. "Looks like we aren't the only ones on a date."

"Out as friends," Sammy corrected, picking up her menu again and looking over the choices. Brock gave a little wave, and Sammy assumed it was to Noah and his date.

"Good evening, you two," Noah said a moment later, as he stood by their table.

"Hello, Pastor Noah," Brock said.

"Hello," Sammy mumbled as she pulled the menu closer and tried to keep her eyes from drifting too far. The thought of meeting the woman who was with Noah made her stomach sour. An image of Noah and Maryann flashed through her mind, and she fought the urge to excuse herself to the restroom.

"Pastor, I hope I'm not being too forward, but I do believe you have the prettiest date in the whole room." Sammy shot Brock an evil look for complementing another woman in front of her, but Brock just smiled at her from across the table as he darted his eyes left.

"Thank you," a little voice said, and Sammy turned to find herself eye to eye with Suzanna. "Hi, Miss Sammy," the little girl said with a huge smile on her face.

"Suzanna," Sammy said with relief. "Don't you look lovely." She was dressed in a pink dress that stopped at her knees with ruffles around the bottom.

"Mama and Daddy went to a play and Jude is with Grandmama, so Uncle Noah and I get some special time just me and him."

"Well, that is special," Sammy agreed.

"We won't keep you," Noah said, the faintest of a grin on his lips, but his blue eyes held an emotion Sammy couldn't place. "We just wanted to say hello. Have a great rest of the evening." He took Suzanna's hand, and they walked back toward the front of the room where the hostess had put them in a booth.

Brock and Sammy placed their orders when their waiter showed up, and then fell into small talk. "So, what are you going to do now that you're out of the Army?" Sammy asked, as she took a sip of water.

"Not sure," Brock answered with a one shoulder shrug. "A friend of mine over in California has been asking about me heading that way and coming to work for him. Mechanics is my first love, but I may also decide to stay around here. Mom and Dad are getting older. My sister Grace is pregnant with her second kid. Might catch up on some old friendships." He shot her a smile. "Who knows what will happen."

"I bet your parents would love having you back," Sammy said. "How are they all doing? I haven't had a chance to talk with them in a few months."

"They're good," he said with a nod. The rest of the evening progressed with easy conversation and good food. By the time they left, Sammy noticed that Noah and Suzanna were already gone. She felt a little disappointed that they hadn't said goodbye, and a little embarrassed that Noah had caught her on a date. *Not a date*, she corrected herself. *Just out as friends.* But Noah didn't know that, and that made her uncomfortable, although she couldn't figure out exactly what bothered her about that.

"You're bothered by it," Lucy whispered the next evening as they made their way through the line for church dinner, "because you like Noah." Sammy quickly looked around to make sure no one was listening to them.

"Keep your voice down," she hissed to her friend. Lucy rolled her eyes and grabbed a glass of sweet tea.

"Look, the only reason you're feeling guilty," Lucy begun but Sammy interrupted.

"I am not feeling guilty. I said I felt uncomfortable." They both stopped and looked around the room to find a place to sit when Brock caught their eyes with a waving hand.

"That's just semantics," Lucy said. "Are we going to sit with him?"

"It would be rude not to, since we've already made eye contact." Lucy sighed and started toward his table.

"Good evening, ladies," Brock said with a wide smile.

"Hello," they said in unison as they sat.

"I could really get use to spending my evenings in the company of beautiful women." He gave them both a smile and then turned his attention to his plate just as Lucy rolled her eyes. Although Sammy had reservations about sitting with Brock, the conversation between the three of them flowed smoothly, and by the time she excused herself from the table, Brock and Lucy were in a deep discussion about a TV show they both watched.

Sammy threw her trash away, then left the fellowship hall. She took a deep breath when the door closed behind her, and she was standing alone in the quiet hallway. She made her way down to the Missions table, where all the current Missions books were. She pulled one out of her purse, checked to make sure she had signed her name and exchanged it with one she hadn't read. She loved the mission books that came out each year. She found it inspiring to read about missionaries out in the world doing great things. She turned around, eyes down as she tucked her new book into her purse. Suddenly she collided with a solid object, and hands came out to steady her. "I'm sorry, Samantha." She found herself looking into familiar bright blue eyes. Noah's hands were still on her upper arms as he spoke. "I didn't see you passing by." Sammy looked behind him and saw Pastor Gene's office.

"No, no," she said, shaking her head and stepping back, a little sad to lose physical contact as Noah let his hands drop away. "I wasn't watching where I was going. Totally my fault." She offered a shaky smile.

"Well, I am glad that I *ran* into you," Noah replied with a smirk.

"Ha, ha, not funny," she offered and had to resist the urge to stick out her tongue like she did with Lucy. She tucked a lose strand of hair behind her ear. "You were looking for me?"

"Yes." Noah left the sentence hanging for a moment, and Sammy's eyes grew wide, and she felt her heart sped up. Clearing his throat, he quickly added, "I, um, just wanted to make sure you were still going to watch Suzanna play ball tomorrow?"

"Of course," Sammy answered. "Wouldn't miss it." She gave a tight smile and pointed down the hallway. "I really need to, you know, get to the sanctuary." She hurried past him.

"Samantha, wait." She stopped, took a calming breath, and turned back. Something in his eyes tugged at her heart, and that scared her. For a long moment, they just looked at each other, and when he didn't speak, Sammy smiled again, turned, and left. Noah blew out a long, heavy sigh and felt a hand clap him on the shoulder as Pastor Gene came up beside him.

"When are you going to ask that girl out, son?" the older gentleman asked.

"It's not that simple," Noah admitted.

"Now, I know I'm an old man," Gene started. "And technology confuses me, and I don't understand the latest fashion trends, but asking a girl out can't be that much different from when I use to do it."

"No, I guess it's not," he agreed, with a smile.

"Then what's the problem?" Noah shook his head and looked over at his new mentor.

"Cowardice," he answered, and then headed down the hallway as well.

"I'll pray for you," Gene said, quietly. He glanced up past the ceiling, right to heaven, smiled and then pulled his door shut. Time to preach.

Chapter 6

Noah sat on a park bench the next afternoon, looking out over a still and peaceful pond. The park was empty and the only sounds he could hear were a gentle breeze rustling the leaves. Yellow and red tulips buds dotted the green grass and the sweet smell of early Spring flowers washed over him. The bright sun hung in a perfectly blue sky without a cloud. He looked down at the sandwich in his hands. When he stopped and bought it, a quiet lunch by himself was just what he wanted. However, now that he was here, by himself, he wasn't sure what he wanted. In fact, it seemed to him that not knowing what he wants was the motto of his life. *God,* he began. *I feel like I'm drifting.* "Good afternoon, Noah." Looking up at the sound of his name, his heart fluttered. Sammy stood with a lunch bag and a smile.

"Samantha," he said, standing up. "What a pleasant surprise. Please, won't you join me?"

"Are you sure?" she asked. "You seemed to be in deep thought. I wouldn't want to interrupt."

"No interruption," he said. "Actually, I would love the company. Sometimes being alone with your own thoughts can be a dangerous thing." He waited until Sammy had sat down on the other side of the bench before sitting as well.

"Kathy came in for a few hours, so I get a rare lunch break," she explained, as she opened her lunch bag. She pulled out a peanut butter and jelly sandwich and began to unwrap it. "I know," she said. "I'm the highest example of fine dining."

"You can't go wrong with a PB&J," Noah replied. They ate in a companionable silence for several minutes. When Sammy had finished her sandwich and pulled out a bag of grapes, she spoke.

"We only went out as friends," she said, not taking her eyes off the ducks in the pond. "Brock and I," she clarified. "We, um, dated back in high school, but we've known each other since we were kids. When he went into the Army, and we lost touch." She finally turned her eyes to his and for a moment, the intensity in them made her forget what she was saying. "We were just out as friends, catching up." She forced herself not to look away as emotions played through his eyes. "I just," she started after a few moments. "I just didn't want you to get the wrong idea about me and him." She felt her face getting hot under his gaze and swallowed down the embarrassment. *What if Lucy is wrong*, she suddenly thought in a panic. What if he really didn't like her? What if she was making a complete fool of herself? She suddenly wished that the earth would open and swallow her up. *Urg! Why do I even care what some stranger thinks?*

"I'm glad," he said, offering his lopsided grin, then rushed on to add, "that you told me."

"Me too." Another moment of quiet passed, and Sammy turned her eyes back to the pond. "And about that comment Brock made, about being my first."

"Sammy, I don't really need details or explanations. We all have a past." *Lord knows that I do*, he thought.

"I know that, but I just want to explain. Rumors get started when people don't clear up misunderstandings. Brock was a lot of firsts for me. He was my first date, my first boyfriend, my first kiss, but it never went any further than that with him." Sammy couldn't say that she had never gone further than kissing with someone, but that was before she became a Christian. That was a whole other life. She was a different person back then. "I've done some pretty dumb things in my life, and some really stupid things before becoming a Christian, but Brock and I, you know, never went that far." She had no idea why she was explaining this, or why she felt it was so important. Sammy glanced over at Noah, sure he must think her crazy or something.

"Like I said, we all have a past, but thank you for telling me." She wasn't sure, but she thought he did look genuinely relieved.

"So, um, did Suzanna have a good time out on the town with you?" she asked, eager to change the subject.

"I think so. I fed her dinner, bought her ice cream, and took her bowling. I mean, it wasn't classy, but she seemed to enjoy herself."

"Oh, I bet she had a wonderful time. That's a memory she'll treasure forever."

"You think?"

"Absolutely," she answered, stuffing her empty grape bag back into her lunch box. "Memories with family is so important, and at her age, being out with someone who's not mama and daddy is a huge deal. I bet she's told all her friends about it." Noah smiled at the thought. "I think you've got another tick mark on the Best Uncle award application."

Sammy waved when she finally saw Noah at the ballfields. He had told her after their unexpected lunch together-where she about died from embarrassment, that Suzanna was playing on Field 3, but it still took her some time to find him. He smiled and stood up as she approached. "I saved you the best seat in the house," he said, indicating the camp chair beside him.

"So very kind of you," she replied, as she sat down and dropped her small cooler. "Have I missed anything?" she asked, turning her eyes to the field.

"Nope, they just started about three minutes ago." For a long time, they both kept their eyes on the field watching the girls. They both cheered when Suzanna got a hit.

"Where's Janet and Ken?" Sammy asked, while the teams switched positions.

"Over by the dugout," Noah answered. "It's a little too noisy over there. All the girls cheering and all the parents yelling." He shook his head. "We can move over there, if you want."

"No, this is fine," she quickly agreed. They talked easily between each other, as they continued to watch the game. Occasionally, Suzanna would wave to them both and they both dutifully wave back. "She looks like she's having a great time. A natural out there."

"She gets that from her mama," Noah said. "Cause

her Uncle Noah sucks at sports. You laugh," he said, looking over at her. "But once I was playing t-ball when I was about her age. I stepped up to the plate, put on my best game face, and when that ball got tossed to me, I swung like the World Series depended on my hit."

"That sounds like an amazing play," Sammy said, entranced by this little piece of his childhood.

"Ah," Noah continued. "You're assuming that I actually hit the ball."

"Still, striking out isn't the end of the world. Especially for a seven-year-old."

"Again," Noah said, shaking his head. "You're assuming. There I was, bat in hand, bases loaded, my whole team cheering for me." He shot her a sly smile. "Ok, maybe we only had one kid on first because no one else had been able to hit the ball, and nobody was cheering because I was the worst player on the team, but that's not as dramatic" Sammy laughed, and Noah went on. "Anyhow, there I was bat in hand, there's the pitch, I swung."

"And?" Sammy asked, leaning over the arm of her chair slightly. Noah did the same.

"The bat flew out of my hands, and hit the helmet of the catcher behind me, bounced off and cracked the coach standing behind him in chin." Sammy quickly covered her mouth as she began to laugh. "Yeah," Noah said, shaking his head. "Blood everywhere. For some reason, I sat out the rest of the season."

"Oh, Noah," Sammy said, reaching out to touch his arm. "I'm sorry. You must have been so disappointed not to play."

"Not really," he answered, covering her hand with his own. "I hated playing sports. After that, my parents at least stopped trying to encourage me to." He shot her another smile, as the crowd began cheering and their attention quickly went to the field. They both stood as Suzanna rounded second, ran past third and slid into home. Everybody continued cheering, as the girl who had hit the ball also made it into home, giving their team a 4 to 2 lead.

"Thank you for inviting me," Sammy said, as they made their way through the crowd after the game. "I had a really good time."

"Thank you for coming. I know Suzanna really liked having you here." Noah glanced over at her. "And so did I." When they made it to her car, Noah propped the chairs against it and turned to face her. His eyes drifted past her, and he raised a hand in greeting. Sammy threw a look over her shoulder and waved to Pastor Gene and Ms. Esther as well. Noah cleared his throat and shoved his hands into his pockets. "So, um, I was wondering," he began. Sammy waited and watched. Noah moved a rock around with the toe of his shoe.

"Good evening you two," Maryann said, walking up to them. She flashed Noah a big smile but directed her words to Sammy. "Sammy, just the person I needed to see. That charity event that we talked about the other day is a go. I'm so excited. So, if it's okay with you, I'll stop by sometime this week to pick up those books?"

"That's great, Maryann. Yes, the books will be ready to go. Either Kathy or I can get them for you."

"Thank you so much," Maryann said, reaching out

to touch Sammy's arm. "This is going to be such an awesome event." She glanced back over at Noah. "Maybe we could get Pastor Noah to donate a little of his musical talents." Noah looked from her to Sammy and back in confusion. "No worries, we'll talk about that later. Oh, I see Mrs. Castleberry," she said with a wave. "Let me go catch her. See you two later." With that, she hurried off.

"What event am I likely to be roped into doing?" Noah asked nervously.

"It's nothing, really. Once a year, we gather up all the eligible bachelors in town and auction them off. Women pay big bucks to have a date with a man of her choice. And some bachelors bring good money. My bet is, you'll be the one everybody is fighting over. A date with the Signing Pastor. Oh, I can see it now." Sammy tried to hold a serious expression, but finally gave into laughter when all the color drained from Noah's face. "I'm joking, I'm joking."

"That's not funny," Noah scolded. He ran a hand through his hair and tried to settle his racing heart.

"Yeah, it was actually," Sammy laughed. "I'm sorry, I just couldn't resist. The event is a charity fundraiser for the local animal shelter. They're gathering items- books, gift cards, stuff like that. I think Maryann just wants you to do a little singing for entertainment." Sammy laughed again at the look of relief on Noah's face. "Anyhow, you were in the middle of saying something before Maryann showed up."

"Ah, yes, umm." Noah rubbed the back of his neck but stopped when he noticed the grin on Sammy's face. *Dang nervous habit,* he thought. "Would you like to go hiking on Saturday? With me?" There, he had done it. It wasn't a romantic date somewhere, but he had stepped out of his comfort zone and asked Sammy to go somewhere with him, other than a T-Ball game.

"Hiking?" Sammy wasn't sure what she was expecting but an invitation to hike wasn't it.

"Yeah, you know, walking through the woods, fighting bugs and ticks while the sun beats down on you. Sweat and mud and sometimes even tears."

"Are you trying to get me to say no, because you're doing a good job at it." Sammy teased, crossing her arms.

"I mean, hiking, that lovely outdoor activity where the sunshine washes over you and you get to commune with nature and if you're lucky, find yourself closer to God." He offered her his crooked grin, but she could still see the worry in his eyes.

"I'm not much of a hiker," she explained. "Last time I went I fell and sprung my ankle." She watched him a moment longer, before adding, "but I think it's time to try it again. Of course, I'll need to see if Kathy can work for me."

"Great," he said. "Can I have your number?" he asked, holding out his phone. "In case something comes up?" She reached out and took his phone, quickly calling herself, before handing it back. "How about we head out around 10? We can pack a picnic lunch."

"Sounds perfect."

"Yes!" Lucy shouted and pumped her hands in the air. "You're going on a date with Noah. It's about time." Sammy couldn't help but smile as her friend danced around the living room.

"Are you done?" She asked from her place on the couch.

"Almost," Lucy said, jogging in one place, her fists shaking up and down in excitement. "Yes, yes, yes!" Lucy took a deep breath, then sat down opposite Sammy on the couch, her feet tucked under her. "Ok, I'm good." Sammy shook her head but laughed.

"And it's not a date," she clarified. "We're going hiking, not exactly a fancy restaurant and candlelight, is it? Just two *friends* going hiking. And what do you mean it's about time? We've only just met."

"Honestly, would you prefer that? Candlelight and fancy?" Sammy thought about it a moment before answering.

"No, not really. I think going hiking is the perfect way to spend a Saturday with Noah."

"I've got to ask," Lucy said, reaching over to the coffee table for her slice of apple pie. "What happened to your reservations about him being a pastor?" Sammy shrugged her shoulders.

"Well, since it's not a *date*, I don't have to worry about that, right?"

"So, you say," Lucy teased, taking a bite of her pie. "Can I ask you something else?"

"Sure, I guess. If you must." Sammy said. "We are best friends, what's on your mind." Lucy took a bite and slowly chewed as she thought.

"What do you have against Noah being a pastor?"

"What do you mean?" Sammy questioned, taking a bite of her own pie.

"Well, I can tell you like him, but you keep refusing to entertain the idea of dating him or even going out on *one* date with him. I was just wondering why?" Again, Sammy didn't answer right away, and Lucy didn't push the subject. After a moment, Sammy put her fork down in her empty plate and turned her eyes to her friend.

"I'm not sure," she said truthfully. "I guess I put pastors at a different level than a normal person," she laughed. "I can't wrap my mind around them dating or kissing or anything. Thinking about it just, I don't know, seems weird."

"You know," Lucy said, with one eyebrow arched in the air, in question. "That Pastor Gene is married, and they have five children, so I'm fairly certain there was some kissing in their lives at some point. A whole lot more than kissing, really."

"Lucy!" Sammy scolded, heat coloring her cheeks.

"I mean, I'm not wrong." Lucy stood and gathered up their empty plates. "Don't think this conversation is over, but I'm going to bed. I've got an early morning. Good night." She disappeared into the kitchen and then returned to grab her water cup before heading to the stairs. After taking a few steps, Lucy stopped and turned back to add, "The fact that you've *thought* enough about kissing a pastor to have an opinion is interesting."

"Lucy!" Sammy clamped her lips together as her friend disappeared up the stairs, her laughter floating down to mock her.

Sammy looked at the clock for what felt like the hundredth time since she got up at six o'clock. "For not a date," Lucy began coming into Sammy's room with a bowl of cereal in her hands. "You sure are nervous."

"Don't start," Sammy warned, sending a glare over. Lucy smiled and took a bite of her cereal.

"So, do you know where you're going hiking?"

"Nope," Sammy answered. "Noah hadn't said." Her phone dinged and she walked to her bed and picked it up. Noah's name flashed on the screen. She slid the button to unlock it and read the text. "Speaking of Noah, he sent a text saying he's on his way." Lucy walked further into Sammy's room and sat down in the chair at Sammy's desk.

"Nice of him to text," she said.

"Yes, it was," Sammy snapped. "Sorry." She flopped on her bed and laid back. "It's just hiking," she said aloud. "Why am I nervous? I mean, he's a *pastor*. What's he gonna do?"

"Sammy, you need to stop thinking of him as only a pastor. First and foremost, he's a man. Don't forget that."

"You're not helping," Sammy groaned, covering her face with her hands.

"And you're overthinking," Lucy said. "You said it yourself. He's becoming a friend. Just relax and enjoy yourself." Sammy let her head fall to the side to look at Lucy. "Oh, and to add to things, Brock sent you flowers."

"What?" Sammy asked, sitting up. "When?"

"They arrived this morning," Lucy answered. "I

was actually coming up here to tell you." Sammy grabbed her phone, stood, and strolled out of her room. She stopped in the doorway leading into the kitchen when a large vase of roses sat on the kitchen table. Sammy carefully approached them like she was afraid they would explode. Reaching out, she plucked the card.

"Hoping to change your mind," she read out loud.

"Two weeks ago, you didn't have a man on your radar," Lucy said around a mouthful of cereal. "Now, you've got two trying to gain your attention." Sammy took a deep breath and let it out, just as the doorbell rang.

"Not a word about the roses to Noah," she threatened.

"Wouldn't dream of it."

Chapter 7

Noah pulled into a parking place in a state park about forty-five minutes from Sammy's house. "Have you hiked here before?" he asked, opening his door, and getting out.

"Once," she answered, coming around to the back of Noah's truck. "But it was a long time ago. And one of the easy trails. I mean, four-year-old kids in flip-flops were passing me." She reached into the bed and pulled out her backpack.

"I'm sure it wasn't that bad."

"It was sad," she joked. "Which trail were you thinking about hiking today?" Noah only smiled as he adjusted his own pack. "How come I'm finding myself becoming suspicious."

"Come on," he said with a jerk of his head. "Let's hit the restrooms and then we'll head out. Got your water?" Sammy held up a full water bottle. "Great."

They slowly walked to the restrooms and once each had had their turn, Noah led them to a trail head marked with a red stripe. "I think you'll like this one," he told Sammy. "But let me know when you need to rest." The hike wasn't hard, but Sammy could tell they were making their way up hill. They talked easily and often stopped for Noah to point out a bird or some kind of fungus. Turned out he was very knowledgeable about all things outdoors. "You do a lot of hiking?" Sammy asked, as they crossed a small bridge. "I bet you were a Boy Scout."

"That obvious?" he questioned with a grin.

"Well, maybe only slightly," she laughed.

"I spent a lot of time hiking when I was younger. It helped to deal with things." Sammy drew her eyebrows together at that comment but didn't press for further information. "I haven't done it in a long time though. Just started getting back into it over the past year or so. And yes, I did spend a little time in the Scouts."

"How much further are we hiking?"

"Not much further, in fact, if you listen, you can hear where we're going." They both stopped and Sammy closed her eyes, letting her ears tune into nature. The sound of water reached her ears and tugged the corners of her mouth up.

"Is that water?"

"Yup. I thought we could have lunch at the waterfall."

"Oh, that sounds perfect," Sammy agreed. They continued walking down the trail and as they came around a bend, Sammy stopped, her eyes wide, her mouth forming an o. The waterfall wasn't the biggest, but it was beautiful. Cascading down the rocky face of the mountain into a blue pool at the base. The grass around the area was green and lush. "It's lovely."

"I'm glad you think so, Samantha," Noah said, watching her as she took in everything. The waterfall, the grass, the flowers. The peacefulness. "Come warmer weather, this is a great place to go swimming. That water never gets too warm, but for right now, it seems we have the place to ourselves."

"How come I've never been here?" Sammy asked more to herself than to Noah.

"Come on, there's a place right over here that's perfect for relaxing." He led her away from the waterfall to a patch of green grass. He pulled a thin blanket from his pack and together, they spread it on the ground. Sitting, Sammy noticed that they had a wonderful view of the waterfall. They went about pulling out their lunches and leaned back on some rocks that were warmed from the sun.

"This place is absolutely perfect," she said, after Noah had offered grace and before taking a bite of her sandwich.

"It's one of my favorite places, for sure. I always feel like God is here, and if I listen, I can hear him talking to me. Kind of like that old hymn." He sang a few lines, and the melody seemed to fit into their surrounding perfectly.

"And what is He saying today?" she asked when he stopped.

"That I've brought great company." Sammy blushed and started on her lunch.

"So did you grow up around here?" she asked after a few minutes of silence. Noah chewed his food slowly as he debated on what he should say.

"Not really," he said, his words guarded. "Our grandparents lived close by, so we spent some time here every summer. Hiked this trail once or twice with my

Granddaddy. How about you? I know you went to school around here, but have you always lived here?" Sammy popped a chip into her mouth, aware that Noah really didn't offer any insight into his past or where he came from. *Interesting*, she thought.

"Yup, born and raised. My parents moved here when they were pregnant with me."

"Do they still live around here?" Noah wondered.

"Naw," Sammy said, shaking her head. "They're retired and bought a RV a few years back. They are currently traveling the US being camp hosts at different state parks. They come back this way a few times a year to visit."

"That sounds like fun." Noah put his trash back into his backpack. "My dad passed away about five years ago and Mama is in Texas helping her sister. Before that she was in Washington with a cousin and before *that* she lived in Florida running a little store." He gave a laugh. "I guess she's kind of like a modern-day gypsy. Never happy in one spot long."

"Did you travel a lot when you and Janet were kids?" She noticed that Noah's motions stopped for a moment before he answered.

"Not really," he finally said. "Janet and Vickie, they are twins by the way, are a bit older than me. So, by the time I came along they were already in school and so we were tired down. Guess Mama is just making up for lost time." They gathered up all their trash and stood. Grabbing their backpacks, Noah glanced up at the sky. "I didn't think it was supposed to rain until late today," he said, nodding to the darkening clouds. "We should get a move on it, if we want to complete the loop before getting wet." They each adjusted their packs, and Noah led them toward the path marked with red.

"What about your dad?" She asked once they were on the trail. "What was he like?" Again, she noticed he wasn't quick to answer, and she wondered about that. The muscle in his jaw worked and he kept his eyes forward. Sammy reached out to touch his arm and stopped walking. "I'm sorry," she said, when he stopped as well. "I didn't mean to ask something that makes you uncomfortable."

"It's okay, Samantha." He took a deep breath. "I just don't really talk about my past or my dad. It's not your fault. It's a fair question."

"But one you don't have to answer. I can tell you about my parents and their crazy dog instead," she offered with a smile that he returned.

"I would love to hear more about your parents," he said. "But first let me answer your question. My dad wasn't a very nice man. I mean, he was somewhat okay when he was sober. He was strict, especially with the girls. He ran a very tight ship, so to speak. But once he started drinking, things got a little rough in the house. Then he got hurt at work when I was about twelve and his drinking became more and more. And so did the abuse, both emotionally and physically."

"Oh, Noah, I'm so sorry." He placed his hand over where hers still rested on his arm.

"It was a long time ago," he told her, clearing his throat. "But the scars are still there. I know Janet doesn't like to speak about it, so if you could please not mention it."

"Of course," Sammy quickly agreed. "Thank you for trusting me."

"Come on," he said. "Let's start walking again, and you can tell me about your family."

By the time they made it back to Noah's truck, the first drops of rain were beginning to fall. "Just throw everything in the cab," he told Sammy as he unlocked her door and pulled it open. He quickly hurried around to open his. They both shoved their packs in, crawled into the seat and closed the doors just as the bottom fell out of the sky and the rain came down in a steady sheet.

"Wow, that was close," Sammy laughed, watching the water drops explode on the windshield.

"As much as I love a rainy night, I'm glad we didn't get caught in this. If you don't mind, I think we'll sit here a few minutes and wait for it to lighten up some."

"Only if I can eat my snack," Sammy answered, reaching for her backpack. "My lunch is completely gone."

"Go right ahead." Noah watched her dig into her bag and after a few moments of searching, she triumphantly pulled out a small bag of homemade trail mix.

After she had eaten a few handfuls, she turned her eyes to the pastor. "Did you always want to be a preacher?"

"Absolutely not," Noah told her without hesitation. "When I was young, I wanted to be only one thing- a superhero." He sat up and struck a superhero pose with his fists on his hips, making Sammy laugh. He smiled over at her. "Then once that dream faded at about, oh, 9 or 10, I wanted to be a rock star." He strummed an air guitar and bobbed his head up and down sending his hair flying.

"You mentioned you played in a band in high school and college," Sammy reminded him.

"Yeah, well, I'll be honest with you, I didn't really finish college. I mean, I did, obviously, because I have a degree in Biblical Studies, but originally, I didn't."

"Why is that?" Sammy waited as she watched raw emotion play across his face. Emotion she couldn't place. She waited.

"I killed someone," he finally said, his voice flat, as lighting lite up the sky and thunder clashed. The warmth in the air got sucked out and time inside the truck cab seemed to stand still for a moment.

"Noah?" Sammy said his name softly, begging for an explanation. For a moment, he stared out of the truck windshield. He seemed to be watching something play out in front of him that Sammy couldn't see.

"I, umm, I wasn't the best kid in the world," he began, his hand coming up to rub the back of his neck. Sammy didn't say anything this time. Instead, she gave him time. "I told you about my dad was a drunk, and well, I turned to drugs to cope." He turned to look at her, his blue eyes clouded with so much grief and hurt that Sammy's heart broke.

"You don't have to tell me," she said, placing a gentle hand on his arm, giving him the option to stop.

"I know," Noah answered with a nod. "But I want you to know. Not many people do. No one around here but Pastor Gene and of course Janet and Ken." He took a breath and licked his lips but stayed quiet. Finally, he began, "I was about fourteen when I started using. Nobody knew, or at least if they did, they didn't say anything. My grades never faltered, and although there were days that I was late or even fell asleep in class, my teachers knew my home life, knew what the girls and I dealt with and they all just- looked over it. Looked over *me*. Easier to ignore me than deal with the situation. I graduated on time and even went on to college. Everything seemed to be falling into place, but drugs and music were the only things that kept me going. I knew it was hurting my mom and my sisters, but it was my escape, you know? And I figured that it wasn't putting anybody but myself in danger. Then towards the end of my first year, a buddy and I were at a party, and someone brought out something harder than what I normally did. I was stoked and didn't think twice about it. I had just broken up with my girlfriend and I thought what the hell. Whatever was going help me cope." He shook his head and took a deep, ragged breath before continuing. "Anyhow, I encouraged my friend to try it too, and when he refused, I jumped in with the other guys making fun of him. Really ragging him about it." He stopped again, and let his eyes drop. "Some friend I turned out to be. He finally gave in and tried it- peer pressure at its finest or worst, depending on how you look at it. Anyway, something went wrong. He had some kind of…allergic reaction. I was too high to know what was happening and by the time I surfaced the next day, he was in a coma." Noah closed his eyes, but tears escaped from under his lashes and rolled down his cheeks. "He never came out of it. He died about a week later."

"Oh, Noah," Sammy said, reaching over and taking his hand, interlacing their fingers. "I'm so sorry, that must have been so hard on you, but you can't blame yourself. That wasn't your fault." Noah shook his head and used his free hand to angrily wipe away the tears. Mad at himself for showing so much emotion. He could still hear his dad's voice calling him weak for crying. Calling him every name he could think of for bringing such a disgrace to the family.

"But it was," he said. "I was the one who took him to that dumb party. I was the one who picked on him. I was the one too high and self-absorbed to call 911." He hit the steering wheel with the palm of his hand. "Of course, I know God has forgiven me, at least on one level I do, but even now, even after these years of being a pastor, I'm not sure how to forgive myself." He took a deep breath; shame of his past constricted his chest. "I bet I sound pretty pathetic right now. There are days when I feel like a fake. How can I minster to others, preach about God's love and forgiveness, if I can't even deal with myself?"

"You don't sound pathetic or like a fake," she answered, giving his hand a squeeze. "You sound like a person with a lot of sorrow. A person still struggling with his past. A person who is doing the best he can." They sat in silence for a few minutes, watching the rain come down all around them. "How did you go from a druggie to a preacher?" she asked tentatively, curiosity getting the better of her. Noah's mouth twitched up on one side and he gave a quick huff of a laugh.

"I was arrested," he said, after taking a ragged breath. "Spent some time in jail and that's when some crazy, bible thumping preacher guy with shaggy grey hair and tattoos all up his arms showed up. Throwing around words like *God loves you* and *Jesus died for your sins*. He was the last person I wanted to talk to, and I tried hiding every time he showed up, but I was 20 years old, disowned by my family, well, by my dad at least, sitting in jail for drugs and feeling guilty about killing my friend and that old geezer just wouldn't go away. He was there every day. When I got out of jail, he was there too. Inviting me to church. Offering me a place to stay. Handing me a bible."

"It sounds like he really believed in you."

"Yeah, a lot more than I believed in myself. So, I went to his house. I went to his church. He helped me get clean, to stay clean. He opened my eyes up to God, that He really did love me. That I really was someone worthy of being loved. I owe him my life." Again, he turned and looked her in the eyes. "And one thing led to another, and boom, here I am. An unemployed worship pastor stuck in a truck with a beautiful woman during a rainstorm." Sammy felt the heat of a blush creep into her cheeks.

"You have a powerful testimony, Noah. You shouldn't be ashamed to share it."

"Who wants a pastor who's an ex-druggie responsible for someone's death?"

"Who wouldn't?" Sammy questioned. "It shows that you're human. That you made mistakes and God still used you for His purpose. Have you thought about how many people you can touch? How many people you can relate to? You've come a long way from that 20-year-old scared, messed up kid. I, for one, need to know that God loves me even though I'm far from perfect. That's what makes Pastor Gene so relatable, he's made mistakes, he's done dumb things, but he still listened to God. He was willing to follow God's plan even when it wasn't what he thought he needed. Sounds a lot like you, huh?" Noah dropped his eyes, while the weight of Sammy's words washed over him. Could he open up about his past? Was that why God had sent him to this little town? Was that why he had been caught in this downpour with a bookstore owner? He took a deep, shaky breath, held it for the count of ten and blew it out, before looking over at the woman next to him.

"Thank you, Samantha," he said, and Sammy saw the dark clouds in his eyes had cleared. "You said a lot of things I needed to hear. Maybe it is time let people see the real me." She returned his smile, before glancing out the window at the clearing storm.

"I think," she began, turning back to Noah, "that sometimes we end up exactly where we need to be to say the right thing to the right person. You're a remarkable person, Noah. Stop standing in your own way. Stop overruling God. Let Him continue to use you."

Noah sat on his bed later that night, his back propped up on pillows, his hair still wet from his shower. He stared at his phone; at the message he had typed out. He had reworded and reread it a dozen times. Finally, he hit the send button.

Noah: I had a great time today. Thank you for going with me. He let his hand and phone drop to his chest, as he laid his head back and closed his eyes. It was a lame message, he knew that, but every time he tried writing more, he felt dumb and needy. A moment later, his phone buzzed.

Sammy: I had a great time too. I'm glad I went.

Noah: I wanted to apologize to you. I know I dropped a lot on you- telling you about my past. There's a reason I keep that to myself.

Sammy: Don't you dare say you're sorry. I'm honored that you trust me enough to share part of yourself. And that's what friends are for, right?

Noah stared at the words. Part of him was ecstatic that Sammy considered them friends. Another part, however, felt like she had punched him in the gut. *I've been friend zoned*, he thought to himself. Did he consider them friends? *Yes, of course.* Did he want more? He wasn't sure. Then why did the words hurt so much? So, he did what he always did when he was confused. He put his cellphone down beside him, rolled off the bed to his knees and prayed.

He wasn't sure how long he knelt there, head bowed, eyes closed, praying- before he felt someone in the room with him. He didn't rush, but eventually ended his prayer, twisted his body, and came to sit cross-legged on the floor. Back to the bed and eye to eye with his sister. Janet sat in the same fashion just inside his door. Neither one of them spoke for a long while. "You told Sammy about your past," she finally said, her words a statement, not a question. Noah didn't answer but averted his eyes. "How did she take it?" Again, Noah was silent, and Janet didn't push him. She just sat and waited. Just like when he was younger, Noah needed time to organize his thoughts.

"Better than I expected," he finally answered, his eyes still focused on his hands.

"Good. It's about time you shared it with her." Janet

smiled when he snapped his eyes up to hers. "Believe it or not, Noah, you do have the right to be happy and Sammy seems to make you happy."

"Janet, don't," he growled, standing up and walking to the window.

"Don't what? Don't want you to be happy? Don't want to see my little brother move on with his life? Oh, maybe don't think you're the best brother ever and a dang good pastor?" Noah turned and faced her once again- his blue eyes hard and cold.

"It's not that easy. First off, I'm leaving in few weeks."

"To do what?" Janet questioned, as she stood as well. "You left your position at your old church. Where are you going to go? Cause nothing is holding you to that other town. And we do have a Worship Pastor position open. You could apply. We would love to have you stay."

"Secondly, Sammy seems to be trying to rekindle what she once had with Brock."

"According to who?" Janet demanded. "Because from what I've heard, yes, she's been out a few times with him as friends, but she's not interested in dating him." Noah pushed a hand through his hair in frustration.

"You just don't get it," he snapped, turning away again.

"Then help me understand," she pleaded.

"Because I'm broken," he shouted, rounding on her in anger. They stared at each other. "I'm broken," he repeated quieter. "I'm a fake. I'm a druggie."

"Recovering druggie," Janet quickly corrected.

"I've spent time in jail. I feel like my whole life is a lie. People call me pastor, but how can that be me? It's like I'm living someone else's life, and at any minute everything is going to crash down around me." He took a breath to try and calm his nerves. His hands clenched into fists. "What do I have to offer anybody? To a church? To you and the kids? To offer Sammy or any other woman out there? Just a broken shell of a man." Tear escaped his eyes and ran down his face. Irritably, he tried brushing them away, only to have them replaced with new ones.

"Oh, Noah," Janet said, moving toward him and wrapping her arms around him. "I'm so sorry. I'm sorry you feel like this and I'm sorry you can't see what we see." She pulled back and put her hands on his upper arms. "Now you listen to me, little brother. You are not a shell, and you are most definitely not a fake. You are one of the most down to earth, real people I know. You are an awesome worship leader and a wonderful pastor. The things you've been through only make you that much more understanding and relatable to people. You are a good person and God has moved in your life so much."

"That's what Sammy said," he said with a soft laugh.

"Then listen to her, and to me. God forgave you a long time ago. He led you to the ministry and you followed. Stop using your past to stop your future. You'll never live up to what God has planned for you if you keep holding your past self as a crutch. You are Pastor Noah Sinclair," Janet said. "And you have the power to help so many people. Start living up to who God says you are, not who you have decided you are. You may leave in two weeks. You may stay. Sammy may not be to woman called to take this journey with you, but if you keep hiding, then you'll never know." She pulled her brother back into a bear hug. "I love you, Noah, but you have to love yourself."

Chapter 8

"You friend zoned him," Lucy accused, as she popped a blueberry in her mouth.

"I did not," Sammy argued, shaking her head. "I simply told him that's what friends are for." Lucy pushed her plate out of the way and banged her head on the table.

"Sammy, Sammy, Sammy," she said with each hit.

"Look, I don't have time for this," Sammy said, getting up and taking her plate to the sink. "I have to get ready for church."

"All I'm saying," Lucy continued as she followed her friend from the kitchen, up the stairs and into her room, "is apparently he poured his heart out to you."

"He did not pour his heart out," Sammy corrected. "He just told me about his past."

"Same difference," Lucy dismissed with a wave of her hand. "And you tell him that's what friends are for, he's going to read that as *friend zoned*." Sammy walked out of her closet holding her outfit and looked at Lucy. Was she right? Had she friend zoned Noah without meaning to?

"But that's not what I meant. At least, that's not what I think I meant."

"Maybe not, but I'll put money down that that's

how he took it. What did he say after you texted that to him?" Sammy dropped her eyes and twisted the soft fabric in her hands.

"He never responded," she murmured. "Oh, my gosh, he did take it like that." Sammy walked over and sat down on her bed.

"Do you like him?" Lucy asked, leaning against the door frame. "Honestly."

"Of course, I do," Sammy snapped. "Didn't I just say we were friends?"

"You know what I mean," Lucy snapped back, unfazed by Sammy's sharp tone.

"Oh, Lucy, I don't know what I feel." Letting out a frustrated sigh, she fell back on her bed. "One part of me thinks he's a great friend. Another part thinks what if we could be more." She draped an arm over her eyes.

"And what about Brock? You've been seeing a lot of him too." Lucy waited for Sammy to answer.

"I'm not sure. Brock and I have a lot of history, but I don't really feel like I use to. He keeps saying he's going to change my mind, but I don't think that'll happen," she said, sitting up again. "How did I get here?"

"You mean to a place where two men are bidding for your attention?"

"What am I going to do?" Lucy walked over and sat beside her friend.

"I think first of all, you need to have a heart to heart with God and let Him do most of the talking." Sammy nodded her agreement. "Then you really need to figure out where you see yourself with both guys. And tell Noah you didn't friend zone him," Lucy added with a giggle.

Sammy stood at the open doorway of Noah's temporary office. He sat in the desk chair, with his back to the door. "Noah," she said, giving a light knock on the frame. "Can we talk?" The chair spun around, and Sammy's breath caught as he stood to greet her. He was dressed in black jeans and a blue button shirt with a black vest. His eyes seemed clearer, bluer somehow and Sammy felt that maybe he could see her soul.

"Samantha, please come in." He gestured to her to take a sit and he came around the desk, turning the second chair to face her.

"Are you ok?" she asked, concerned. "You seem… different. Not quite yourself." Noah smiled, and she realized she had never seen him fully smile, only that little crooked grin he's so fond of doing. This smile lit up his whole face, it showed off the dimples in his right cheek, and it made her smile back at him.

"I'm wonderful," he answered. "And to the contrary, I feel more like myself than I've felt in years. God and I had a long talk last night. I feel like a great weight has been lifted from my soul and off my shoulders."

"That's fantastic," she said, reaching out a hand to touch his arm. A wave of heat shot through her when he covered her hand with his, surprising her. "Lucy suggested I needed to do that as well." Noah's brows drew together in worry.

"What's wrong," he asked. "Is there anything I can do to help?"

"Not really," she answered, shaking her head. "Just some personal stuff." She looked around the small office, buying some time before looking back over at Noah. "About last night," she began. "When I said we were friends."

"I was excited to know that you consider us friends," he interrupted. "Especially after such a short time and everything I dropped on you. It really was unfair to you. I'm truly sorry about that."

"Yes, well, about that. I didn't mean to say that we were friends, I mean, not that we aren't, but I didn't mean to imply that we could be friends. Only, that is." Sammy felt like an idiot. She suddenly stood, too nervous and embarrassed to stay seated near him. "I mean, we are friends and all, but I feel like that needed to be clarified." Noah watched as she paced back and forth across his office. When she finally stopped Noah stood and took a step toward her.

"I'm afraid you're not making much sense right now, Samantha."

"I know," she admitted, swallowing hard. After a deep breath, she continued. "As Lucy would say, I didn't mean to *friend zone* you." There. She had said it. Now it was out in the open between them and she had no place to run and hide, she did, however, worry her bottom lip between her teeth. The intensity of his gaze made her uncomfortable, and her heart race all at once.

"I must admit," he began. "It did feel like you threw up the friend barrier last night." He took another slow step toward her.

"I really didn't mean it as a barrier," she said,

resisting the urge to step backwards. Her voice sounded breathless to her own ears, and she cleared her throat. "I do consider us friends, it's just, you know. I should be going." She tried to step around him, but Noah didn't move. Instead, he dropped his gaze to her mouth, and then back up to her eyes. Sammy licked her lips and tried to swallow to wet her suddenly dry throat.

"Have lunch with me today," he said, softly.

"I'm sorry," she whispered. "I'm afraid I already told Brock I'll eat with him and his family after church." She could barely force the sentence out of her mouth. It felt like she had just slapped him. However, Noah didn't flinch, but she saw emotion cloud over his blue eyes. Was that jealousy? Before she had time to process what she saw, a knock on the door frame broke the spell. "I'll talk to you later, Pastor Noah." She quickly gathered her items and slipped past Pastor Gene out of the office, not meeting the other man's eyes and forcing herself not to glance back.

"Well, now," the older gentleman said with a hint of laughter to his voice. Noah turned to face the senior pastor, who he thought was trying hard not to smirk. "I know that look. To quote the younger folks, you've got it pretty bad for our Miss Sammy." Gene stepped further into the office and closed the door. "We've only got a minute before we need to get going, but I've got to ask, son, what are your intentions? Cause Brock has his sights set on that pretty young lady as well, and I don't want to see her heartbroken." Noah walked over to his desk and picked up a file folder. He stared at it for a long moment before he turned back to Gene and held it out.

"I have a few requests," he said, as Gene took the

folder. "First, keep it as quiet as you can for two weeks. Second, let me give my testimony to the congregation before the board interviews me." Pastor Gene opened the folder and smiled when he read over the application for full time Worship Leader and Associate Pastor. "I want to be the one who tells Sammy and I think the whole church should know who I really am." Pastor Gene closed the folder and smiled at Noah.

"In that case, Noah, I'm praying that you can win her heart."

Now that Noah has made up his mind to stay, or at least try to stay, the church still had to accept his application and offer him the job, he felt lighter than he had in years. With his application turned in, and his secret safe for two more weeks, his goal now was to figure out how Sammy actually felt about him. To see if he stood a chance against her high school sweetheart. He knew that memories were a powerful thing, and sometimes our own sugar-coated memories could be dangerous to the present. He pushed open the door to By the Book bookstore and walked into the silent shop. The cool air surrounded him in a welcome hug. "Samantha," he called out.

"What a lovely surprise," Sammy said with a smile as she walked out of the back room carrying a box of books. "I wasn't expecting to see you today." After their conversation yesterday, and Sammy having lunch with Brock, she thought that Noah would choose to stay away a few days. *Or forever.*

"I brought you some coffee." He held out a cup to her. She sat the box on the counter and reached out for the cup. Their fingers brushed as she took it, and a spark flew up Sammy's arm. She quickly pulled away, wrapping both hands around the cup.

"Thank you." She took a sip and closed her eyes with pleasure. "That's just what I needed today." When she opened her eyes back up, she found Noah watching her- one side of his mouth crocked up in a half smile.

"How was your lunch with Brock?" he asked, taking a seat. She watched him for a moment over the rim of her cup as she took another sip.

"It was good," she finally said. "But do you really care about how my lunch went?"

"We are friends," he replied. The corners of his lips twitched letting her know he was trying not to laugh. Sammy tossed her ponytail over her shoulder and narrowed her eyes at him. Something was going on with him, she just couldn't figure out what it was. "I did stop by for a purpose, though, and you're right, it's not to talk about Brock. I was wondering if you'll like to go out to dinner with me tomorrow night?" The question stopped the ascent of Sammy's cup to her mouth.

"Dinner?' she questioned. "With you? Like a date?"

"Should I be offended by the way you said that?" Before she could answer, the bell above the door chimed.

"Welcome to By the Book," she began, her eyes still held captive by Noah's teasing gaze.

"Just me, Sammy, no need to be formal." Brock made his way over where she stood, backside propped against the front counter. With a smile, he leaned in and gave her a kiss on the cheek. Sammy saw Noah's jaw flex, and watched his eyes go dark. *Was that jealousy on his face? Hadn't she seen that look yesterday at church?* "'Sup, Pastor Noah," Brock said with a lift of his chin, then turned his attention back to Sammy. "Dang, you look hot today." Sammy glanced down at her jeans and t-shirt. "I can't stay long, I just wanted to come by and see if you wanted to hang out tomorrow night?"

"Hang out?" Sammy drew her eyebrows together. *What are we, 15?*

"Yeah, me and Kevin and Sally- a group of us- are meeting down at Two Lick Cow for trivia night at eight. And we all know how smart you are, you use to rock trivia nights." He gave a deep laugh, before continuing, "Even when we weren't old enough to be there. Anyhow, what do you say?"

"Thanks for the offer, but I've already got plans for tomorrow." She glanced over at Noah and noticed a small smirk on his face before he lifted his coffee cup to take a sip.

"Come on, Sammy," Brock pleaded. "It'll be fun."

"I'm sure," she answered looking back at him. "But like I said, I've got plans and I don't want to change them." Brock gave a defeated sigh.

"Alright. Well, if your plans *do* change, you know where to find me. I'd still love to see you. I've got to get going. See you around. Bye Pastor."

"What are you smirking about?" she asked the moment the door closed behind Brock.

"Me? Smirking?" Noah asked with feigned innocence. Sammy laughed at his wide eyes and shocked expression.

"You don't like Brock, do you?" she asked as Noah stood and threw away his empty cup. Her breath caught when he took a step toward her. Lifting her eyes slightly to look directly into his, she felt her heart slam against her chest. His eyes were dark with emotion, and this time Sammy could easily read what it was.

"It's not a matter of not liking him," Noah said. "He seems like a great guy. It's a matter of us both wanting the same thing." Sammy felt her knees go weak and was happy she was leaning against the counter. They stood like that for a moment before he took a step away. "I'll pick you up at seven. Nothing fancy, just whatever is comfy." Sammy nodded, not trusting her voice, and he smiled. "See you then, Samantha." With that, he left the store, and Sammy felt the air get colder in his absence. Reaching behind her, she gripped the counter to help support herself and willed her racing heart to slow down.

"You've really got to stop doing that," Sammy said, with her hands over her ears. Lucy had just let out a scream that Sammy was sure would have the neighbors calling the cops.

"Well, I'm sorry," Lucy said, a huge smile on her face. "It's just that you are giving me so many reasons to be happy." She started dancing around the room in wild, crazy movements- stopping occasionally to throw in more recognizable moves such as the Charleston, the Running Man and the Floss.

"Wow, those dance lessons are really paying off." Lucy flopped down on the couch and threw a pillow that Sammy easily caught.

"You can joke all you want, but this is big, no huge, no, it's gigantic. No, no, I've got it, it's enormously colossal."

"Fairly certain those all mean the same thing," Sammy laughed.

"Fine, act like that." Lucy shrugged. "I'm just happy that my bestest friend in the whole wide world has finally stepped outside her comfort zone and is going out on a date with a very kind and smart and caring man. Not to mention handsome as sin."

"Lucy," Sammy snapped, throwing the pillow back.

"Ok, ok, I think it's out of my system- for now at least." Lucy drew her knees up and wrapped her arms around them. "So, when are you going out?"

"Tomorrow. He said it's not fancy. I texted him this afternoon and asked where we were going but he wouldn't say."

"Has to be better than Two Lick Cow." Lucy made a face. "I mean, I like the place okay, their hamburgers are the best, but everybody knows going after eight just means a bunch of rednecks drinking. I can't believe Brock asked you to go there."

"He was just remembering when we used to go. Before he left."

"I know, but still," Lucy wrinkled her nose. "Anyhow, I'm so glad you said yes to Noah."

"Why are you so happy about me going out with Noah?" Sammy asked. "You've been rooting for this from that first day he walked into my bookstore."

"I don't know," Lucy answered. "I just think you

two would be cute together." She gave a one shoulder shrug. "When you're with Brock, you seem to always be holding back part of yourself. Even back when we were younger. But with Noah, it's hard to explain. You seem-yourself."

"I'll have to think about that, but for now, I'm heading to bed. Good night."

Sammy had just slipped into bed with her current book when her phone dinged.

Noah: *What did the scarecrow preacher say to his congregation?*

Sammy: *I don't know, what?*

Noah: *Can I get a Hay-man.*

Sammy: *That was so corny.*

Noah: *What did Jonah's family say when he told them about what had happened before reaching Nineveh?*

Sammy: *Do I want to know?*

Noah: *Hmmm...sounds fishy.*

Sammy: *booooo....*

A moment after she sent the last message, her phone rang. She smiled when Noah's name popped up on the screen. "Couldn't type fast enough to tell me all your bad jokes?" she asked answering the phone.

"What do you mean, bad jokes? Those where laugh out loud funny."

"More like groan out loud." Sammy rolled her eyes

even though Noah couldn't see her. "Please tell me you really didn't call to tell me more jokes." She heard Noah chuckle on the other end.

"I do have a ton of jokes, but no, I didn't call to tell you my whole joke collection. We'll save that for other day."

"Wonderful," Sammy deadpanned.

"I called to ask if we could do 7:30 instead of 7 tomorrow. Pastor Gene wants me to go with him the nursing home to visit with a few of the church's older members. He wants me to sing a few hymns for them. I don't think we'll be back until close to 6:30. I'm sorry." He did sound sorry.

"Of course, I don't mind," Sammy said. "I know they'll love hearing you sing. You have such a lovely voice. And if you meet someone named Mrs. Lilly Jones, tell her hello for me. She was my Sunday School teacher when I was little. Ninety-four and still going strong."

"Absolutely and you sure you don't mind?" Sammy could hear the worry in his voice.

"No way, but maybe you could do me a favor. You know, something to make up for me having to wait an extra thirty minutes for dinner."

"And what do you want, Samantha?" Noah's voice was low and deep. A shiver ran down her spine. *That's a dangerous question.* She had mentioned the favor as a joke, but now it had taken on a whole different meaning.

"I don't know yet," she answered, trying to keep

her voice calm and the conversation light. "I'll think about it and get back to you."

"Fair enough, I suppose. I'll let you get back to your book." Sammy glanced down at the book beside her.

"How did…how did you know I had a book handy?" Again, Noah chuckled, and Sammy felt her skin prickle with goose bumps.

"Call it a lucky guess. Good night, Samantha."

"Good night, Noah."

Chapter 9

Sammy glanced up at the clock on the wall and let out an aggravated sigh. Time was ticking by slowly, and she was going crazy. Kathy was coming in at 4 o'clock to give her plenty of time to go home and get ready for her date. *Her date. With Noah.* That thought still made her stomach do a little flip. Turning her eyes back to the computer screen, she finished double checking her order before hitting the submit button. She was just about to click into Solitaire when the bell over the door chimed. "Welcome to," she stopped when she saw it was Brock walking up to her.

"Hey, Sammy," he said with a smile. "I thought I would swing by and see if your plans have changed. I would really like it if you came down to Two Lick Cow."

"Sorry, I still have plans," Sammy answered. "But I do appreciate you thinking of me." Brock folded his arms on the counter and leaned forward with a smile.

"I think about you a lot," he told her. His eyes raking down her body. Before Sammy could formulate a reply, the bell chimed, and Kathy walked in.

"Sorry I'm a little late," the other lady started. "I got held up by a tractor. Oh, hello, Brock."

"Hey, Kathy. Look, Sammy, just keep me in mind if your plans change." He gave her a wink, said goodbye to

Kathy and headed to the door.

"I'm so excited that you have a date," Kathy started, as the door swung shut.

"Why is everybody so excited?" Sammy questioned. "It's not like I don't date. I went out with Brock last week." Ok, maybe that wasn't the best example to use. She gathered her belongings and came around the counter.

"Of course, dear," Kathy purred, "but this is different. *This* is Pastor Noah." Sammy groaned and rolled her eyes.

"You sound just like Lucy," she said. "Do you two have Pastor Noah Fan Club meetings?"

"No, of course not" Kathy said, grinning. "But that's a great idea." Sammy shook her head.

"Goodbye, Kathy," she said, walking out the door as laughter followed her. She hadn't walked far when Brock fell into step with her.

"Did I hear Kathy say you have a date?" he asked, hands shoved into his pockets.

"I suppose you did," Sammy answered, keeping her eyes looking forward.

"I must admit, I'm a little surprised."

"Surprised?" Sammy questioned, coming to a stop.

"No, no, not surprised you have a date," Brock quickly corrected. "Just that, well, I mean, I thought we were going out." He motioned between the two of them. Sammy started walking again.

"Brock, we are not teenagers. Going out a few time-as friends, I might add, does not mean we are exclusive."

"But we use to be," he said. "We used to be in love." Sammy stopped walking again and turned to face him.

"Brock, that was a long time ago. Back when we *were* teenagers. Back when I thought you hung the moon. Back before you left." Sammy almost regretted the words when she saw Brock physically flinch. "Like I said, it was a long time ago. We were different people back then. You can't believe that we could have a relationship based on who we were and what we felt. And I'm not sure love is the right word to use. More like infatuated."

"Then go out with me again," Brock plead. "And not as friends. Let's get to know each other again. Maybe rekindle some of that searing passion we use to have." He smiled at her. "And it was searing."

"I'll think about it," Sammy finally answered. "But I can't make any promises."

"I'll take it," Brock said. He put a hand on her arm as she started to turn to go. "Tell me, who are you going out with tonight?"

"That's not really any of your business," she told him.

"Does mystery man know that you and I went out last week?"

"What does that have to do with anything?" she questioned.

"Ah, well, you see. If he knows about me, then it's only fair for me to know about him. So, I can size up my competition." Sammy's breath caught. Hadn't Noah said something similar. *It's a matter of us both wanting the same thing.* Did she really have two men interested in her? *Of course not.* Things like that didn't happen to a 30-something bookstore owner. *Did they?* She caught her bottom lip between her teeth and reached up and tucked a stray piece of hair behind her ear.

"Alright," Sammy answered, titling her chin slightly up. "I suppose that's a fair point."

"Thank you," Brock said.

"Tonight, I'm having dinner with Noah."

"*Noah?*" Brock asked, and his tone of voice made her instantly irritated. "As in *Pastor* Noah?" He let out a little laugh.

"Why is that funny?" she demanded. Brock smiled and rocked back on his heels.

"I'm not laughing because it's funny," he said. "I'm laughing with relief. Ain't much of a competition, is it? I mean, me against Preacher man."

"Goodbye, Brock," Sammy said, and continued down the street.

"I wish I was there," Lucy said from Sammy's bedroom door. She stood with bare feet, a bowl of cereal in her hands, and her hair pulled up in a messy bun. "I would have punched him right on the nose." To emphasize, she took a big bite of cereal and crunched it loudly.

"Yes, I bet you would have." Sammy laughed as she brushed out her hair and then looked at herself in the mirror. "What I don't get," she continued, "is why do I have two guys suddenly interested in me? I mean, look at you. You look drop dead gorgeous in cutoff jeans and a messy bun, so why me? You should be the one in this mess."

"Girlfriend," Lucy said, her tone laced with irritation. "You are *beautiful*. Why won't you believe that? And beyond your looks, you are smart, and kind, and serving, and funny. Do I need to go on and are you really wearing that?" Sammy looked at her outfit- a faded pair of jeans, a white fitted t-shirt with a burgundy-colored bell sleeve laced cardigan over it, and her favorite pair of cowboy boots.

"What's wrong with it?" she asked, suddenly nervous.

"Nothing," Lucy said with a smile. "I just hope you plan on wearing your black pearls with it."

"Don't scare me like that," Sammy said, but went to her jewelry box and pulled out her pearls. Just as she fastened the strand around her neck, the doorbell rang.

"Show time," Lucy said through a grin. Sammy led the way down the stairs and into the living room, where Lucy took a sit on the couch, legs tucked under her. Sammy stuck out her tongue at her friend for good measure, took a deep breath to steady herself, and then opened the door.

"This is for you," Noah said, holding out a potted plant.

"A plant?" Sammy asked, eyebrows drawn together in question.

"It's a Golden Pothos," he clarified. "It's supposed to symbolize following your dreams and since you followed your dream to open a bookstore, I thought it was appropriate." Sammy looked from the plant to Noah and back. "Plus, cut flowers would die in a couple of weeks, hopefully this will live for years." He smiled when her eyes came back to his. "Although I'm getting a little nervous. Did I make a mistake?"

"No," Sammy quickly told him. "No, not at all." She took the plant and motioned him to come in. "In fact, I don't think anybody has ever put that much thought into buying flowers for me before. That was truly kind of you." She waved a hand toward Lucy. "You remember my best friend, Lucy, right?"

"Of course," Noah said with a smile. "How are you? The last we talked; you were considering opening your own store. How is that going? Wasn't it a Christian gift shop?" Lucy smiled from her place on the couch.

"I'm very well, thank you for asking. And I'm still talking with the bank about getting a business loan, so I'm not giving up."

"I'm glad to hear that," Noah said as Sammy placed the potted plant on one of the side tables, grabbed her purse, and turned to him. "Are you ready?"

"Absolutely."

"Have a good time, you two crazy kids. I won't wait up," Lucy called out just before Sammy closed the front door.

"Sorry about her," Sammy apologized. "She thinks she's funny."

"No worries," he answered, as he led the way down to his truck. He opened the passenger door and offered his hand to help her up. "You look lovely tonight," he said, as she slid in. Before he closed the door, he caught a glimpse of red staining her cheeks.

Sammy had time to take in Noah as he walked around the front of the truck. He was wearing jeans and a button-down black shirt with a design in silver thread, much like the outfit she had first saw him in. She offered him a smile when he climbed in beside her. "So where are we going to?" she asked.

"You'll see," he answered, and cranked his truck up. "By the way, I ran into Brock this afternoon," he threw out, as he backed out of the driveway.

"Urg." Sammy dropped her head into her hands. "I knew I shouldn't have told him."

"He threw down the gauntlet, so to speak." Sammy's head popped up and she swung worried eyes toward him.

"He didn't? What did he do? What did he say? I am so sorry. Oh, how embarrassing." Noah gave a deep chuckle.

"He did indeed. I won't bore you with the details, but I get the feeling he wasn't very happy about us going out tonight. And why are you embarrassed?"

"I hadn't planned on telling him about going out tonight, but he pulled that whole *sizing up the competition* thing. I had no idea he would track you down." Again, she buried her face into her hands. "I'm pretty sure I'm dying over here. How are you with funerals?"

"Sammy don't worry about it. Guys have been doing this for hundreds of years. We're used to it. And are you embarrassed about him tracking me down or that you agreed to a date with a pastor?" He glanced over at her and then back to the road. "Actually, we'll discuss that later," he said quickly, not giving her time to answer. They rode in silence for the next few minutes. Sammy stared out the window at the passing scenery, when she noticed that they were leaving the lights of town behind.

"Where *are* we going?" she asked again.

"Trust," Noah answered. "Trust is a beautiful thing."

"I trust a lot of things. I trust the sun to rise. I trust God to take care of me. I trust Lucy to squeal too loud at good news, but good-looking pastors in bright yellow trucks driving me to an undisclosed location...umm... low on the trust meter."

"Good-looking, huh?" Noah teased with a smile, as he turned off the main road.

"I mean, according to Lucy, anyhow."

"Lucy, huh? So, what you're saying is I might have asked out the wrong roommate?"

"I didn't say that" Sammy answered a little too quickly, and felt heat raise in her cheeks.

"You're blushing, aren't you?" When she didn't answer, Noah laughed causing even more heat to rise.

"I'm not talking to you until we get to wherever you are taking me," she huffed, crossing her arms over her chest.

"Well, don't clam up now, because we're here." Noah had turned onto a dirt road while they talked and bumped his way down towards a small creek. Sammy looked out the front windshield and gasped. Ahead of them, twinkling fairy lights were strung up between three large oak trees. Between them and the bright full moon, she could see the small table with two chairs sitting underneath.

"Oh, Noah, it's lovely," Sammy said, her hands covering her mouth. "You did this?" she asked, turning wide eyes to him.

"I hope this is okay?" Noah pulled off to the side and then backed the truck up to the lights. "I didn't feel like fighting a crowd or having Brock crash the party."

"It's perfect." Noah gave her a big smile, before getting out and coming around to open her door.

"Let's hope you still think that once you taste the food." He led her to one of the chairs, and then dropped the tailgate of his truck. He pulled two coolers toward him. Opening the first one, he pulled out two glasses and a container of liquid. "Sweet tea," he said, placing the glasses on the table and pouring them each a glass. Closing that cooler, he opened the second. "It's not the fanciest place setting, but I had to keep everything hot." He pulled out a tin plate covered in foil. He uncovered it and placed it in front of her.

"Oh my gosh, Noah, this looks- and smells delicious."

"Thank you very much. It's Tuscan Chicken, and it happens to be one of my favorite dishes."

"Did you make it?" she asked, as he pulled out a second plate and sat it in front of his seat.

"Do I get bonus points if I say yes?"

"*Did* you make it?"

"Yes, as a matter of fact, I did. I did buy the bread," he said, pulling out a loaf. He put the top back on the cooler, grabbed a couple napkins with forks and knives wrapped inside, and took the seat across from Sammy.

"Noah, this is," she stopped and looked around-lost for words.

"Speechless? I bet that doesn't happen often." He held out his hands and she tentatively took them. He gave her a smile before bowing his head to say grace. Noah waited nervously for Sammy to take the first bite and felt a wave of pride when she closed her eyes and mmmed.

"That is so good."

"I'm glad you like it," he answered with a smile. They ate in silence for a few minutes before Noah took a drink of his tea and asked, "Ok, what's the most unusual thing you've ever done?" Sammy stopped with her fork halfway to her mouth, and slowly lowered it.

"Did Lucy lend you her *questions to ask on a date* book?" she teased.

"Is that really a thing?"

"Oh, it really is. Ummm, I'm not sure I've ever done anything unusual. I'm pretty common."

"I don't believe that for a minute," Noah answered.

"That I haven't done anything unusual?"

"That you're common. I find you pretty amazing." Sammy dropped her eyes, but he noticed the corners of her mouth tug upwards.

"Ok, I do have something. I was in a duck herding competition when I was a teenager."

"A what? You're joking."

"I'm absolutely serious," she said. "It was the craziest thing ever. My partner and I lost, but it was interesting. And it was for charity, so I guess it was worth all the duck poop." Noah laughed.

"I'll have to look up what duck herding looks like."

"Ok," she said. "My turn. Why did you ask me out?"

"Ah, well, that doesn't seem like it's on the same par as the most unusual thing you've ever done. That's more of a soul-searching question."

"Are you trying to get out of answering it?" Sammy asked, taking a bite of chicken.

"Not at all. I would be lying if I said I didn't find you attractive." He loved how she blushed at every complement. "After our talk in the truck after hiking, I had a heart to heart with Janet." He stopped and licked his lips. "She said a lot of the same things you did. About me holding on to a lot of guilt that I shouldn't have been. That I can't say that I've asked God for forgiveness and then not really accept it. I was lying to myself, and to everybody else. Mostly I wasn't truly doing God's work. After she left, I had a heart to heart with God. He wasn't as nice as you and Janet were. He told me to get up out of my pity party." He shook his head. "I woke up the next morning feeling like I've been given a new life. And I don't want to waste it." Sammy opened her mouth and then closed it. For a moment, they simply looked at each other.

"And you, decided asking me out was part of this new life?" she finally asked.

"I decided that I wasn't going to punish myself

anymore for something I couldn't control. I thought I couldn't be happy because I was betraying the memory of my friend." She nodded understandingly. "And I realized that I couldn't keep holding people at arm's length."

"I'm glad God had a stern talking to you," she said. "And I'm glad you asked me out." As they finished eating, the conversation flowed easily from one topic to another. Once they were done, Noah cleared the table and pulled out two pieces of cheesecake. "How much do you have in those coolers of yours?" Sammy asked.

"I've got a few smaller snacks, but this is the last main thing." He took his seat again and waited for Sammy to take her first bite before saying, "Ok, my turn and the question of the night is, embarrassed Brock came to see me or that you agreed to go out with a pastor?" Sammy's eyes shot up to meet his. He gave a slow nod. "I figured it was the latter."

"It's not really embarrassment," Sammy began. "It's just, I mean." She stopped and dropped her eyes to her cheesecake.

"It's ok, Samantha. I know that my profession is hard for some women to get over. I do like you, and I'm happy that you agreed to come out with me, and I cherish you as a friend, but if you would rather."

"No," Sammy interrupted. "I mean, yes, I'll admit, I did- I do, find the fact you're a pastor a little, not off putting, but." She stopped and took a deep breath. "I guess I always thought of pastors as, you know, already married. I never imagined they, you know, dated." She felt her cheeks grow warm.

"Last time I checked, dating was kind of the

precursor of marriage. Gene and Esther dated."

"Yes, but that was before he became a pastor," Sammy countered.

"The point is, Sammy, I don't want you to be uncomfortable. I would love to take you out again. I know Brock asked you out as well. I don't want to put pressure on you. My job isn't going to change. This is what God called me to do. Being a pastor comes with the whole Noah package. And whoever I happen to end up with, is going to have to have a similar calling. Being a pastor's wife isn't for the faint of heart. Even dating a pastor can be stressful." Sammy watched him from across the table. She looked at the twinkling lights and listened to the sound of the water in the creek.

"Noah, I'm having a wonderful time, and if a certain pastor asked me out again, I'm fairly certain the answer would be yes."

"Just fairly certain?" Noah asked with a grin. Sammy smiled back and continued eating her dessert. Once the cheesecake was done, they worked together to clear the table.

"So how did you know about this place? And how do those lights working without electricity? And aren't you worried someone will take your stuff?" Noah closed the top of the cooler and turned to Sammy.

"So full of questions," he laughed. He took her hand and tugged her away from the lighted area. "Come on, you've got to see the creek. And to answer your questions, they are solar lights. Ken's family owns this land, and I come out with him and Janet and the kids sometimes when I visit." They walked down to the creek side and stopped. The full moon above reflected off the water.

"It's lovely," Sammy said.

"Sure is." She glanced over at Noah and found him looking at her.

"I meant the river," she said, knocking his shoulder with hers.

"I know." He turned to face her, and she matched his movements.

"What's that on the tree?" she asked, nodding to the tall oak that stood guard behind him. In the moonlight she could just make out something different on the trunk of the tree.

"One of life's great mysteries," Noah told her. He pulled out his phone, tuned on the flashlight and led her over to the tree. Shining his light, she could see a heart with the initials G.H. plus E.M. inside a heart. "It's been here forever, and while I don't really approve of damaging a tree, there's something romantic about it."

"True," Sammy agreed, as they walked, hand in hand, back out into the silvery moonlight. "Thank you for this evening. It's been wonderful."

"It's been beyond wonderful. Thank you for agreeing to come out with me." Sammy's breath caught when Noah reached up and tucked a strand of hair behind her ear, and then let the back of his fingers skim over her cheek.

"I just want you to know," he began, dropping his hand to his side, "that I want nothing more than to kiss you right now."

"You do?" Sammy said breathlessly.

"But please don't be offended that I'm not going to."

"You're not?" She drew her brows together in confusion. Noah tightened his grip on her hand.

"Samantha, you are an amazing woman and I want to get to know every part that makes you Sammy. Rest assured, I'm going to kiss you one day, but I want the first time I kiss you to be as amazing as you."

"This *is* a pretty amazing place," Sammy said indicating their surroundings with her eyes. "And it's been a pretty amazing date." Noah smiled as he brought her hand to his lips and pressed a kiss to her palm. Sammy drew in a sharp breath at how intimate it felt.

"Trust me on this, Samantha."

Sammy looked at the picture on her phone and sighed. She knew she was grinning like a fool. Her and Noah took the selfie last night, sitting on the tail gate of his truck. They were both smiling, and Noah had his arm around her back as he leaned in to fit in the frame. She could still smell his cologne. Feel the warmth of his breath. And that kiss to her palm. Sammy looked at her hand and resisted the urge to bring it to her face. When the bell over the door dinged, Sammy swiped up on her phone, and placed it face down beside her. "Welcome to By the Book."

"Just me, sugar," Brock said. "Have a good time last night?"

"Yes, I did," she answered. "Thank you for asking."

"Good, good." He nodded his head. "So where did you go?" Sammy raised an eyebrow at him. "You're right, I didn't come here to talk about Pastor Noah. I came to talk about you. And me. Going out tomorrow night."

"Tomorrow? Where?"

"Ah, now I want that to be a surprise." Sammy crossed her arms over her chest and glared.

"You know that I don't do surprises."

"Ok, fine. There's an outdoor concert next town over," he told her. "Some local groups playing Rock 'n' Roll from the fifties and sixties. They're going to have food trucks out and I thought it would be a fun evening." Sammy watched him for a moment. "What do you say?"

"I don't know," she answered, tentatively. "It does sound like fun."

"We'll have a great time. Come on, say yes." Sammy pondered the invitation for a moment longer. She had said she would think about a more-than-friends outing. And an outdoor concert *did* sound like a lot of fun.

"Ok," she agreed. "I'll go."

"Yes, great. Why don't I pick you up around six from here?" Sammy nodded her agreement and Brock's smile grew. "Awesome. I'll see you tonight at church."

"Interesting," Kathy said, coming up to the counter. "Last night there was Noah and tomorrow there's Brock. How many more guys you got hidden up your sleeve?" Sammy rolled her eyes and began gathering her stuff. "I mean, a few weeks ago, you weren't dating anybody. Now, you've got two handsome guys are your beck and call."

"Now you know full well that's not the case. And I'm not dating either one. I just happen to be going out on a date with each."

"Still interesting," Kathy said again. "All I know is that sooner or later, you'll need to make a choice and I don't envy you on that."

Chapter 10

Lucy grabbed Sammy's elbow and steered her to a table in the back of the fellowship hall. "This way," she said. "Those men of yours will get the point that tonight, you're mine."

"They aren't mine," Sammy countered. "Anyhow, I don't see either one."

"See?" Lucy said, stabbing her plastic fork in Sammy's direction. "You've already looked. And one of them *could* be yours if you played your cards right."

"I've been thinking about that."

"Oh no." Lucy thumped one of her elbows down on the table and dropped her head into her upturned palms. "Please stop doing that. You're going to say something incredible sensible, aren't you?" Sammy gave her friend an apologetic smile.

"Afraid so and it's about Noah. You know as well as I do that he's only here for another week or two. If something did develop between us, what do we do then?"

"First of all, what do you mean *if* something developed? From what you told me about last night, something has already developed. And you don't know, maybe he'll stay?" Lucy suggested. "Or maybe you could go with him?"

"Leave my store?" Sammy stopped eating and looked at Lucy.

"You've got Kathy to help run it, and me. It's doable." Sammy caught her bottom lip between her teeth as she thought. She loved her store and had worked hard to get it up and running. Could she leave it to follow a man on a maybe dream?

"Good evening, ladies," a raspy voice said, bringing their attention to Pastor Gene.

"You don't sound so good," Lucy stated.

"I know," he agreed. "A little too much cheering at my grandson's t-ball game, I guess."

"Going a be kind of hard to preach sounding like that."

"Indeed. Good thing Pastor Noah is going to be taking the wheel tonight." He smiled at the women. "In fact, I was wondering if one of you young ladies could grab him a little bit of food and take it to him? Poor guy is so nervous I don't think he's come and gotten anything."

"Don't you worry, Pastor," Lucy said with a smile. "Sammy is about finished; she'll head that way right now. I would, of course, but I promised to help with clean up tonight." Gene smiled and patted Sammy on the shoulder.

"Thank you so much, dear. Now if I could only find, ah there he is. Excuse me." Pastor Gene walked off and Sammy noticed he intercepted Brock as he walked in the door.

"Now, you," Lucy said, taking Sammy uneaten pimento cheese sandwich and wrapping it in a napkin, "take this and that bottle of water and go while Pastor has

Brock cornered."

"Are you two in on this together?" she questioned.

"Don't be silly. I just know when a fantastic opportunity has been laid before you. Now go."

"We are having a serious talk later," Sammy hissed, as she gathered her items and the sandwich, then hurried out. She took a deep breath and before she knocked on the closed door of Noah's office. When he saw her through the window, he stood and waved her in. "I'm sorry to interrupt," she said, opening the door. "But I didn't see you in the fellowship hall and Pastor said you were preaching tonight, and well, I thought you might be hungry." She held up her offerings.

"That's very kind of you. Please come in." Sammy walked in, leaving the door open. "Won't you have a seat," he said, taking the sandwich and water from her.

"Oh, no, you're busy. I don't want to intrude."

"Please? Talk to me while I eat. Maybe it'll help with my nerves." Sammy placed her purse and Bible in one chair while sitting in the second. Once she was sitting, Noah took his seat again and began to unwrap the sandwich.

"You do look a little green around the gills," Sammy said with a playful grin.

"Thanks for pointing that out," he said, taking a bite. After he swallowed, he continued. "I've had about two hours to prepare. I'm a Worship Pastor. I can lead singing for hours, but I'm not too experienced in preaching a full sermon. Don't tell anybody."

"Don't worry so much, Noah. I'm sure you'll do

fine." She nodded toward his open Bible and notepad. "You seem to have some notes, so you've prepared something." Noah shook his head as he took a drink of water.

"That's just it," he told her. "I've been working on something, but every time I go back over it, it just doesn't feel right. It's like I'm missing something." He propped his elbows on the desk and buried his head in his hands. "I think being a professional duck herder may be my new calling in life." Sammy barked out a laugh, and quickly covered her mouth.

"I'm sorry. I don't mean to laugh at your stress. Maybe you need to forget about the notes, and just let God lead you. Pastor Gene often goes at it without notes."

"Pastor Gene has been doing this for a few more years than I have," Noah pointed out.

"Just a thought," Sammy said with a shrug. "Can I pray for you?" His eyes found hers in gratitude.

"I would love that." Sammy scooted forward in her chair and reached out for his hands, which he gladly gave.

"Dear Heavenly Father," she began, closing her eyes.

Outside the door, Pastor Gene smiled down at his wife. He placed a hand on the small of her back and moved them down the hall. "A couple that prays together, stays together," Esther whispered.

"God put that boy here for a reason," Gene responded. "And He crossed their paths for a reason too. I haven't seen two people who belong together more than those two… since us, of course, my love." Esther smiled up at her husband and gave him a playful jab in the gut.

"Nice save there at the end," she said with a chuckle. "But I agree, those two are meant to be, I just hope they'll figure it out."

"I don't doubt they feel it," Gene told her. "I'm just worried that Sammy will feel tied here and to her store and the Noah will feel like he needs to move on." Esther put her hand on his arm.

"I guess time will tell. And just look at us. We figured it out."

Noah finished the worship part of the evening a little too fast for his liking. As he put down his guitar, the words that Sammy prayed came back to him. Looking out over the people looking at him, he sought out her face and smiled when he found her. Taking a deep breath, he laid a hand on his Bible, and began. "I had a sermon wrote out for tonight, but no matter how many times to read it and rewrote it, it just never felt right." He stepped away from the pulpit, thankful that he opted for the portable lapel microphone. He walked down the stairs to stand on the floor in front of the congregation. "But a very smart person gave me some very faithful advice." He paused for a moment. "So, I ask you, why not?" And with those words, Noah dove into a sermon of why not take a chance, why not chase you dreams, why not live your life for God the way He was leading you too? He walked while he talked, moving from one side of the room to the other. He paused to tell a story from time to time that started out random but ended with the same message he was preaching on. Often, he had the whole church laughing at his shenanigans and nodding their heads with his words.

By the time he said the closing prayer, the room was alive with electricity. The spirit of God could be felt by each heart.

Sammy wanted to stand up and cheer. Noah had ditched his notes, preached from his heart and he rocked it. As people started to file up to the front to shake his hand, his eyes sought hers out, and when they met, she gave him a huge smile, which he returned, before he had to turn away to greet someone. She gathered her items, and as she went to stand, Brock called out her name. "I was hoping I would see you. We still on for tomorrow night, right?" He looked hopeful and half afraid.

"Of course. I'll be ready at six just like we talked about."

"Awesome. Hey, can I walk you to your car?" Sammy had to force herself not to cast a glance over at Noah, before giving her answer.

"That would be nice, but how about you walk me to the Adult Sunday School room instead? I have a meeting to attend."

"Whatever my lady wishes," he said with a smile and a small bow. Sammy rolled her eyes, and scooted past him, leading the way to the door. She could feel Noah's eyes on her, and she chanced a quick look in his direction before walking out the door.

"Noah, my boy," Pastor Gene said, slapping him on the back. "That was an excellent sermon. Excellent. I had no idea that you had that in you."

"To be honest, I didn't either, Pastor. But sometimes, the right person says the right thing." Pastor Gene smiled at him.

"That they do," he said following the path of Noah's gaze. "I would ask who, but I have a feeling I know." Gene patted him on the back once more. "I've been praying for you, son."

"Thank you." Noah watched the older man walk away and looked around the now empty room. He took a deep breath, turned, and went to his knees at the altar. "Thank you, Lord," he whispered. "Thank you for being here. Thank you for giving me the right words." He didn't know how long he stayed on his knees praying, before he heard the soft sound of footsteps and then felt someone kneel beside him. Still, he didn't open his eyes. He knew who it was, and he knew she would understand. After a few more moments, he ended his prayer, leaned back, and looked at Sammy. Her head was still bowed, and he enjoyed the moment of just watching her. When she opened her eyes and looked at him, his breath caught. What was it about this woman that made him feel alive? That made him want to do better. Be better. A better man. A better pastor. Better everything.

"You did a wonderful job tonight," she said. Noah stood and offered his hand to help her up.

"I couldn't have done it without you, your words and your prayer." They stood where they were for a moment, and Sammy watched an array of emotions play through his eyes.

"It was all you and God," she answered, pointing to him and then up beyond the ceiling.

"Are you here alone? Has Lucy already left?" He wanted to ask about Brock, but felt it really wasn't his place. Sammy smiled but didn't call him out that she knew what he was asking.

"Lucy left right after our meeting. I was heading out when I noticed you were still here. I seem to always keep interrupting you while you pray. I'm sorry."

"Then next time, we'll pray together." He watched her for a moment, like he wanted to say more. "Can I walk you to your car?"

"I'll like that," she answered. They made a quick stop by Noah's temporary office to pick up his bag, and then he held the door open for her as they made their way out into the almost abandoned parking lot. Sammy noticed the Pastor Gene's car was still parked in his normal space, along with Mrs. Tucker's car and Julie Cunningham's truck. "How's Janet and the kids? I didn't see they at church tonight."

"Jude wasn't feeling too good. Janet's taking him to the doctor tomorrow, but she's fairly certain he has an ear infection."

"Oh no. Please let them know I asked about them."

"I will." They stopped at her car, and he waited while she unlocked and opened her door. She tossed her stuff in her seat and then stood to face him.

"Well."

"Well," he repeated.

"I should probably get going. I have an early morning and a long day."

"Of course." Sammy paused for another moment, before turning to her car. "Sammy," Noah started again, causing her to turn back. "I was wondering, what are you doing Saturday morning?" She cocked her head to the side.

"It depends. What do you have in mind?" Noah gave her one of his lopsided grins.

"It's a secret, but I was hoping you'll still agree to accompany me on my mission."

"Suspicious yet intriguing." Sammy crossed her arms. "Tell me more."

"I'm afraid I can't give you too much info. Top secret. Very hush-hush."

"Now, that's funny. Because I was pretty certain preachers are supposed to be on the up and up."

"We are," he said and then leaned in toward her and her heart skipped a beat. "But every once in a while, we like to take on top secret missions." He gave her a wink that made her breath catch. "So, what do you say? I promise you won't regret it."

"I don't like surprises. In fact, I made Brock tell me where we were going tomorrow." She stopped short. She hadn't intended to tell Noah about her outing with Brock. She bit her lip and saw his eyes darken. His Adam apple bobbed as he swallowed, but he didn't question.

"Sometimes, surprises can be fun. You liked the last one. Trust me." There was that word again- trust. Something Sammy didn't do very well when it came to her heart. He gave her a full-blown smile and her knees went weak. "Please?"

"Ok. I can see if Kathy will work Saturday morning. I'll text you tomorrow and let you know."

Saturday morning, Sammy stood in her bathroom

brushing out her hair. Her mind was hopping around to everything that had happened that week. First to the date with Noah, and how perfectly romantic it was. To praying with him before his impressive Wednesday night sermon. She played over her outing with Brock. *Why can't I refer to that as a date?* She even replayed the kiss they had shared when he dropped her off. It was nice, but not the explosion of hormones she remembered from when they were younger. She reached up and touched her lips. In fact, the whole kiss felt a little...*dull*. She looked at her palm and remembered the feel of Noah's lips pressed against it. The spot still felt like it was on fire. She curled her fingers up into her palm, like she was trying to hold on to the feeling. "Oh my gosh," she said aloud to her reflection. "I'm falling for the preacher."

"What was that?" Lucy called from the other side of the door.

"Nothing," she quickly said, and opened the door. "What are you doing in my room?"

"Not guilty." Lucy held up her hands in surrender. "I just came to tell you that Noah is here."

"What?" Sammy looked at her clock. "I didn't hear the doorbell." She hurried to her closet and started pulling things out.

"I was outside working the flowerbed when he drove up. No need to ring the bell. He's waiting downstairs. No hurry. I'll keep him company." Lucy shot her an evil smile, then retreated from the room.

"That's what I'm worried about," she mumbled to herself. She hurriedly dressed in jeans and a t-shirt with a picture of a woman surrounded by books and the words

Just a girl and her books. Throwing her hair up in a ponytail, she slipped on sandals and headed toward the living room where she heard Lucy laughing.

"Oh, my goodness," her friend gasped. "Tell me they didn't catch you there in your boxers?" Sammy stopped just out of view, eager to hear the answer.

"Of course not. I hid in the cabinet under the sink. So, they found my friend, Kevin passed out in pink underwear and a cowboy hat." Lucy hooted with laughter. "But Kevin being Kevin, played the whole thing off as his idea, his *solo* idea. He was sent home early but became the hero of summer camp."

"That's a story that I've just got to hear one day," Sammy said, walking into the living room. Noah automatically stood from his seat. She liked that about him. Lucy wiped the tears from her eyes and fanned herself.

"Noah, that really did make my day. Oh my." Noah smiled at her and then Sammy.

"Always willing to help," he said. "Sammy, you look amazing. Are you ready?"

"Absolutely. Bye, Lucy." As they walked down the steps, Sammy ventured to ask, "So Special Agent Sinclair, what exactly is our mission today?" Noah opened the passenger door for her but didn't answer. He jogged around the front of the truck and climbed in.

"What are your feelings on karaoke?" he asked, cranking up the engine.

"Karaoke? You're kidding?" He just smiled at her and backed out of the driveway.

Sammy laughed as Mrs. Lilly Jones held a microphone in one hand and swung her other in a jerky motion trying to keep beat with the song she had chosen. The wheelchair she sat in bounced slightly, but she didn't seem to mind. The ninety-four-year-old woman belted out the words so loud, she really didn't really need the microphone. Sammy clapped her hands and let out a whoop along with the rest of the room when the old woman finished.

"Mrs. Jones," Sammy started, as she walked up to the stage "That was so awesome."

"Oh my," the retired Sunday School teacher exclaimed breathlessly. "I haven't had this much fun in years. Charles," she called to one of the other residents. "You're next." A heavy-set man with tattoos covering his arms and a limp when he walked started making his way up.

"Only if you promise to sing a duet with me before the day is through."

"Deal." She handed him the microphone and Sammy pushed her off the stage as Noah went about helping Charles select a song. "That's a mighty fine young man you've managed to snag." Sammy felt her face turn red as she parked the chair and put on the brake.

"Oh, we aren't dating," she clarified. "Just friends." Mrs. Jones looked at Sammy and then over at Noah and back.

"Last *friend* I had that looked at me like that, I married. For sixty-eight years he was by my side."

"Mr. Jones was a special man," Sammy agreed, as

she sat down beside her. "But Noah and I are just friends." *Weren't they?*

"Just friends, huh?"

"Just friends," Sammy agreed.

"So, what's holding you back from being more?" Sammy looked over at the other woman and thought about the question. What was holding her back?

"Biggest thing is, he's leaving in a few weeks. I've known from the start that he was only here a short time."

"Sammy, dear," Mrs. Jones said, placing a hand on her knee. "He may or may not be *the one*, but you'll never know if you're afraid to put your heart on the line. What if he leaves? What's to say you can't go with him? What's to say he won't decide to stay here?"

"You make it sound so easy."

"Child, it is easy. It's your mind making it difficult." Sammy glanced back over at Noah, who was laughing at something Charles had said. Was it really that simple? "Love isn't always by the book," Mrs. Jones grinned.

"I see what you did there," Sammy teased.

"I'm serious, though," she laughed. "Love isn't always sweet. Isn't always easy. Isn't always rose petals and romantic walks. Sometimes love is hard. It's messy. It's putting someone else completely before yourself. It's sour milk and burnt dinner, but love- true love- is always, *always* worth it." Sammy watched Noah pat the other man on the shoulder, touched the screen to control the music and then turned to make his way to her. Over the speakers YMCA started playing and the whole room exploded in laughter.

"That lasted a lot longer than I thought it would," Noah said, closing the tail gate on his truck.

"I think they would have kept going, except the nurses said it was lunch time." Sammy laughed as she remembered the groans from the residents.

"They sure are a lively bunch, especially that Mrs. Jones. I see why you like her so much."

"She made Sunday School exciting." Sammy walked over and sat down on the bumper with a sigh.

"What's wrong?" Noah asked, coping her pose. "If you're sad you didn't get a chance to sing, I can set up the equipment at your house. I bet Lucy would love that." Sammy laughed at the thought.

"Don't you dare. The neighbors would call the cops for sure then. No, I'm okay with not singing. I'm just thinking about something Mrs. Jones said."

"Do you want to talk about it? You may not know this, but I'm a fairly good listener."

"Only fairly good?" Sammy teased, knocking into his shoulder.

"Didn't want to overstate my qualifications. I mean, I am a guy, and we aren't known for our listening skills."

"I'm not sure a pastor should go around telling people that."

"What? Did you say something?" Again, Sammy laughed. "I'm serious, though. I'm here if you need to talk."

"I know, it's just, well, it's kind of personal." Noah gave a nod but didn't say anything. Instead, he reached over and took her hand, holding it in silence. After a few minutes, Sammy gave it a squeeze, hopped up and smiled. "Come on. I'm hungry and I know a great little pizza place nearby."

"Sounds like a delicious plan."

After they ate, Noah swung by Janet's house to unload the karaoke stuff, and then they drove down to an out of the way ice cream shop. They sat outside enjoying the warm weather and their cool treats. "You know," Noah began after taking a few bites of his ice cream. "You can tell a lot about someone by their favorite flavor of ice cream."

"Oh, you can, can you? Like what?" Noah took another bite of his while he watched Sammy eat hers.

"Like someone who's favorite is vanilla is graceful, well rounded, they have an understated classic quality about them."

"How about chocolate?" Sammy asked with a smile.

"Ah, well, chocolate says you enjoy life, like to step outside your comfort zone, enjoy exploring new ideas."

"Mint chocolate chip?" She knew she was egging him on but was curious to see what he would say when they got to her favorite.

"What's not to like about the *cool* minty personality of the person who loves mint chocolate chip? He's popular. The life of the party."

"You are so making this stuff up?" Sammy accused, pointing her spoon at him.

"I am not. Honest, there's research about this stuff. I can email you links if you like."

"Ok, how about your favorite flavor?"

"Peanut butter cup," he said, holding his hands out toward his bowl. "It says I'm strong, I put a lot of pressure on myself, but I love to inspire others. And that I'm also handsome and humble." He flashed her a grin that made her laugh.

"Not sure about that humble part," she giggled. "Ok, I'll bite. What does mine say about me?"

"Coffee? Umm, if I remember correctly, it says that you love to read, you have a lot of wisdom and insight to offer people. And you like to go out with with humble, handsome pastors." Sammy had to put a hand up to cover her mouth as she laughed. "Ok, maybe I elaborated at the end a tad bit, but I think it's a fair statement."

"What am I going to do with you?"

"Spend the rest of the day with me?" he offered. She brought her eyes up to his. "I mean, it's already four. What's a few more hours? Maybe grab some dinner? Didn't you say Lucy was working the bookshop this afternoon?" She watched him as he finished off his bowl of ice cream. She liked that he didn't put any pressure on her to make a quick decision.

"And what did you have in mind to do in the hours between now and dinner?" A slow smile spread across his face, and Sammy wondered what she had gotten herself into.

Chapter 11

"What is this place?" Sammy asked, as they pulled up to a large warehouse later that afternoon.

"This is the current homebase of Comfort in the Chaos Ministry." Noah turned off the engine and undid his seatbelt.

"And what is that?" She questioned as she got out of the truck. He came around to her side before answering.

"Currently they pack meals to hand out to homeless people. Tonight, they are heading out to the streets and need help getting everything ready."

"How is it that you've only been in town a few weeks and know about this and I don't?" Noah gave her a smile.

"I've got connections. Goes along with being a secret agent." He gave a laugh when she swatted at his arm. "Okay, the guy that runs it was a buddy of mine back in college...well, that one year I was there, before everything went crazy. Just so happens, he's from the area." He grabbed her hand and tugged her after him as he started walking. "You're going to love these people."

Sammy didn't know making peanut butter and jelly sandwiches and packing them in paper sacks could be so much fun. And Noah had been right, the people inside were great people, and they accepted her right away. She had a great time joking with everybody, and she really felt like she was doing some good in the world. The guy who had started the ministry, Gary Harris, was a lot of fun and had all kinds of stories about a younger Noah. He was always careful never to mention Noah's drug addiction, although he did talk about his openly. His fiancé, Rose, worked at the bank Sammy used, and recognized her right away. Altogether, there were seven people helping out with the food, but as the afternoon ticked away, all but Sammy, Noah, Gary and Rose left for different reasons. "How did Comfort in the Chaos come about?" Sammy asked, as they finished up the last of the sandwiches and packed the last of the meal bags.

"Great question," Gary answered. He hopped up on one of the tables and took a swig of his water. "This part of the ministry started to take root after I spent some time homeless as a teenager. My family fell on some tough times, and before we knew it, we were living out of our car. Luckily, it wasn't long, six or seven months, but I remember how hungry I was."

"Once he graduated college," Rose picked the story up. "He wanted some way to give back. We came up with handing out food to the local homeless, and well, that all led to this."

"That's awesome, but you said *this part*. What else does Chaos do?"

"Another great question." This time it was Noah who answered. "Gary and I are currently talking with Pastor Gene and the board about opening up the Comfort in the Chaos Closet."

"What's that?" Sammy questioned before taking a drink from her own water bottle.

"The idea," Rose said, "came from watching my older sister be a foster parent. They would get calls at all times of day and night for urgent placements. They didn't always have the right gear or even the right size clothes, so they would be stuck scrambling to get things before the new kid would arrive."

"The Comfort in the Chaos Closet," Gary continued, "would be stocked with clothes and furniture and gear and even gift cards. Then when a foster family needs something they could call us, and we could provide it free of charge."

"That's so awesome," Sammy said.

"And it would be a great ministry opportunity for the church to help guide and pray with people," Noah threw in. "A wonderful outreach program."

"Why hasn't the congregation been told about this?" Sammy asked, looking over at Noah.

"Because the board hasn't decided to support it yet," he answered honestly, with a shrug.

"They are a little nervous that Gary and I aren't members of the church," Rose told her.

"Yeah, our church is a lot smaller and one town over. We wanted a church that was more central to everybody, so we sought out a sister church," Gary threw in.

"But since Chaos isn't currently associated with *any* church," Rose continued, "then we are hoping that won't be a stopping point. We are our own non-profit."

"Ok, so what else is holding things up?" Sammy asked.

"We need someone to be our contact person at your church. A Head of Department, if you will, and also volunteers willing to help run it."

"That should be easy," Sammy answered. "I would help. I know Lucy would too."

"Then maybe you would like to come to the next board meeting and share your enthusiasm," Noah suggested.

"Yes, absolutely."

"It's time to start loading up," Rose said looking at her watch.

"How many people are going out tonight to hand out the food?" Sammy asked.

"Just four of us," Gary offered, sliding down off the table. "The other two should be here soon. They are coming from a school play, that's why they aren't here to help pack. A lot of our people had obligations tonight. But we've done it before."

"You two can join us if you want," Rose tossed out as they placed the finished bags into boxes to be loaded.

"I'm afraid I promised Sammy dinner in exchange for her help tonight," Noah quickly answered, not wanting Sammy to feel like she was being pressured.

"But couldn't we go help and then eat?" Sammy questioned, turning toward him. Noah glanced up at Gary and Rose who had both diverted their eyes elsewhere.

"Sammy," Noah said softly, "Gary and Rose understand that we already have plans. They didn't even know I was bringing you tonight."

"Did you already have plans to help tonight?" Noah swallowed and pinched his lips together.

"Yes," he finally said.

"Then I suggest, Pastor Noah, that you start helping Gary load up those bags, because we are going to help." She crossed her arms and gave him a stern look. He leaned in slightly and lowered his voice even more.

"Coffee ice cream also means you're stubborn," he teased.

"Look who's talking," Gary commented with a laugh.

"Get a move on it, brother," Noah said, as he tossed a crumpled bag at him. "These boxes won't load themselves."

By the time all the bags were handed out, and Gary and Rose had dropped Noah and Sammy back off at Noah's truck, it was already nine o'clock. "I am so tired," Sammy said, as she waved goodbye to the other two and leaned against the truck. "But I had so much fun. Thank you for bringing me here."

"Thank you for helping so much. I really didn't expect you to go out tonight. I had talked to Gary already and he was fine with me skipping out."

"How often have you been out with them since you've been in town?" Sammy wondered.

"I don't know, six or seven times," he answered

with a shrug.

"And you're the one who came up with bringing Chaos to our church, aren't you?"

"There was already talk about it," Noah said. "I just, I don't know, gave it a little push."

"And you never once thought to tell me about it?"

"Of course, I have thought about it, but it's hard to ask a girl out and then suggest they hand out sandwiches to the homeless. It doesn't really scream romantic or anything, does it?"

"Fair point," Sammy said. "Still, you could have at least told me about them and what they do." She pushed herself off the truck, then poked him in the chest. "Also, I'm not any ordinary girl." Noah caught her hand and pressed it over his heart.

"Oh, I definitely know that," he said. Sammy's breath caught as his eyes searched hers. He reached up with his free hand and cupped her face. Sammy licked her lips, and his eyes went to her mouth and then back to her eyes. "You, Samantha, are far from ordinary. In fact, I would say you're quite extraordinary."

"Isn't that from a book or movie or something?"

"It was really cliché, wasn't it?" he said, laughing.

"Yes, Pastor Sinclair, I would even call it *extra*-cliché."

"Maybe so, but I meant it. Sammy, you are unlike anybody else I've ever met."

"Is that a good thing?"

"I think so." They stood there a minute longer. The stars twinkling above, her hand over his heart. "Why don't we go get that dinner I owe you?"

"Sounds great." He reached around her and opened the door, bringing his lips even closer to hers. Her heart slammed against her chest, and she prayed that he couldn't hear it. When he stood straight again, he brought her hand to his lips and pressed a kiss to her palm, and like the first time, fire exploded along her nerves.

"You sure were out late," Lucy said, as Sammy walked into the kitchen the next morning. Lucy watched her over the rim of her coffee cup as Sammy moved around the kitchen, pouring her own cup of coffee.

"Yup."

"Spend the whole time with Noah?" Sammy didn't answer right away. Instead, she cut a piece of cinnamon coffee cake, and took it and her coffee to the kitchen table.

"As a matter of fact, I did." Lucy's eyes brightened with mischief.

"Are you going to tell me the details?" Sammy gave her friend a sly smile as she took a bite of her cake, chewing very slowly. "Come on. Spill."

"There's nothing to really spill," Sammy said with a chuckle. "Our day started out setting up karaoke at the retirement home that Mrs. Jones is at. Then we grabbed lunch and ice cream."

"Not sounding like the hottest date around," Lucy commented, rolling her eyes. "Just when that boy was starting to win points."

"It wasn't a date. But it was an awesome day. He

introduced me to Gary Harris and his ministry called Comfort in the Chaos. We helped make bagged meals that we then delivered to the homeless. Oh, and just wait until I tell you all about their plans to help foster parents, but I'll get to that later. Then we went out for waffles." She laughed at the memories that were warming her heart.

"Ok, that does sound right up your alley. And what about kissing? Any movement on that front?"

"Lucy, there's more important things then how good a someone can kiss."

"True," Lucy agreed. "But it sure does help. Tell me this- has Brock kissed you?" At the blush on Sammy's face, Lucy squealed. "He has! And?"

"You're hopeless. Like a 15-year-old girl."

"Umm, the fact that you won't tell me, tells me that he wasn't good." With a sigh, Sammy sat her coffee down.

"It was okay. Lukewarm. Not like I remember it from when we were younger."

"So, in other words, it didn't rock your world?"

"Fifteen *may* be giving you too much credit," Sammy teased.

"I'm serious. Look, you're my best friend. You have two handsome guys chasing you."

"I thought you didn't like Brock?" Sammy threw out, as she got up to rinse her plate.

"Never said he wasn't good looking. Just not as good looking as Noah. My point is- I don't want you to miss out on a chance of happiness. Noah and Brock have been laid back about you going out with both of them, but you're going to have to make a choice." Lucy stood and walked over to her. "You have to figure out what Samantha Felton wants. What is important to you? Where do you see your life and which one- Noah or Brock, is going to fit in better with your life plan?"

"Life plan? You've been reading self-help books again."

"Laugh all you want, but have you talked about kids with either? Church? That one's kind of obvious with Noah. Where do you want to live? Money? Do they mind a working wife, or do they want you to stay home with the kids?"

"Hold your horses, Lucy, I've only been out on a couple of dates with both."

"But wouldn't knowing where each guy stood help you out?" Lucy gave her a hug. "Just think about it."

Sammy stood talking to Carla, Julie and Jasmine about the Women's Retreat that was happening in the Fall. The ladies always collected money to help out those who couldn't afford to go, and they were planning some fundraisers for the summer. She was just about to make her excuse to leave when Noah approached the small group. "Good morning, ladies," he said with a smile. Jasmine was first to speak.

"Good morning, Pastor Noah," she purred. "Loved your sermon Wednesday night, any chance of a repeat?"

"I'm afraid not. Pastor Gene has his voice back and he's ready to go."

"It was wonderful," Julie agreed, before placing

her hand on Jasmine's arm. "Jasmine, would you mind coming to the Woman's Ministry room for a moment? We want to redecorate and could use some help picking out paint." Jasmine eyed Noah one last time, before nodding.

"Of course," she said. "Sammy, we'll talk more later." Noah nodded his goodbyes as the two women hurried off down the hall.

"Is it me?" Noah asked. "Do I smell?" Sammy laughed and shook her head.

"Did you want to see me?"

"Always," he answered in a low voice. "Can we talk in my office?" She nodded and followed him the short distance. He motioned for her to take a seat and then rounded the desk and sat opposite. "Gary wanted to know if we would like to help out tomorrow night with delivering food. The normal group can't make it, and him and Rose need a couple more bodies for safety." The fact that Gary had asked for both of them didn't go unnoticed by Sammy.

"I would love too, but that didn't need a special trip to your office to ask." Noah cleared his throat and tugged at the collar of his shirt. She was about to tease him about his coloring when a knock on his door drew their attention.

"Sorry to interrupt," Brock said, "but I was hoping to talk to Sammy before service started." Sammy looked at him standing at the door and then back to Noah. She could see the muscles in his jaw working and when he looked at her, she saw the irritation in his eyes.

"I'll let Gary know that you're willing to help, and I'll text you the time," he said.

"We'll talk later then." She gave him an apologetic look, gathered her items, and stood. Brock stepped back to allow her to pass by him, before giving Noah a curt nod and leaving the doorway.

Noah stood for a moment in silence, guitar slung over him, and his hand positioned to play. He had picked out the songs last week and Pastor Gene had agreed that it was a wonderful set. Yet as he stood there, looking out over the crowd, watching Sammy as she sat between Brock and Lucy, something in his soul began to stir. He glanced over at the senior pastor who seemed to know he was in a silent battle, because the older man nodded his agreement. "I had a set of songs picked out," he began, pulling the strap of the guitar over his head and placing it on its stand. "However, as I'm standing here, looking out over you all, I'm being led to change my plan. So, I hope it's okay with Pastor Gene that instead of the songs he approved, I'll like to sing to you one of my own creations." He sent a nervous look back to Sammy and made his way over the piano. The man in the sound booth hurriedly got the microphone by the piano turned on and Noah licked his lips before continuing. "I don't normally sing my own stuff, and I hope I remember all the words." His fingers touched the keys of the piano and a few soft notes drifted up into the air. "But mostly I pray that this song means as much to you as it does to me." With that he started playing the first few notes to a silent congregation. His voice soon joined the music, and the blend was hauntingly beautiful. The song talked about mistakes made, lives changed, forgiveness given, and chances taken. Noah's voice floated over the pews in perfection. Finally, the last notes faded away, and Noah sat there, eyes closed- letting God talk to his soul.

"Pastor." Someone called out from the back, and Noah opened his eyes. "If you don't mind, may I talk?"

"Of course," Noah said, standing from the bench and turning to fully face the direction of the voice.

"My name is Jack, and I can't tell you how that song touched me." Jack went on to give his testimony. What he had done as a young man, and what lead him to God. It was powerful and touching, and it made Noah proud that God had worked through his song. After Jack sat down, another person stood up. Pastor Gene made his way to the stage and gave Noah a hug.

"Good job, my boy," he whispered, then turned his attention to the person speaking. After two more people had stood to talk, Pastor Gene approached the microphone. "Anybody else want to give their testimony? I'm serious, if you don't talk, I'll start preaching." That sent a small ripple of laughter through the crowd, but had the desire affect. Person after person stood and gave their testimony. By the time the last person stood, it was twenty minutes after noon, but no one was bothered by the delay. In fact, many stood talking, or at the altar praying long past one o'clock.

"That was amazing," Noah said, when the last person had left, and it was just him and Pastor Gene. As he sat down on the steps of the stage, he smiled at the older man.

"That was all because of you," Gene answered, sitting down beside him. "You and God did that. We haven't had an altar that full in years. And the testimonies." Gene shook his head. "Never in all my years, has it lasted the whole service and beyond. It seems to me that song of yours was personal."

"I wrote that not long after I got the call to be a pastor. God told me to walk away from the old me, and He made me something more. And still, it took all these years, and coming here, to fully understand. To give up the guilt I was holding on to." Noah looked around the small sanctuary. It felt like home, and that made him nervous.

"Is this such a bad place to settle down?" Gene asked, as if reading his thoughts. "God has been talking to you something fierce since you've arrived. And I know one young lady who seems to have her eyes on you." Noah blushed at the comment.

"It's complicated with Sammy," he said.

"Yes, I suppose it is. I also see that Brock is trying to win her back, but I'm not sure if that's for their tomorrows or their yesterdays. They dated a long time back when they were young, but they are both different people now. But I'm just an old man, who's hungry, so I'm not sure what I know." He grunted as he stood from the steps. "You're doing good work here, Noah. I'm happy that you chose to put in your application, but I pray that whatever happens, it's because you listened to a higher power than yourself." Gene patted his shoulder, and then left him sitting alone.

Chapter 12

"You seem to have something on your mind tonight," Noah said, as he and Sammy drove out to the warehouse Monday night.

"What?" Sammy whipped her head around to look at him. "I'm sorry, what did you say?"

"I said that I'm joining the circus and was wondering if you wanted to be the other half of my trapeze act." Noah gave her a grin. "We could call ourselves the Flying Leap of Faith."

"That is *not* what you said."

"Then why did you ask?"

"Because I didn't hear you, but I *know* that's not what you said." Noah laughed at her logic.

"I said that you seem to have something on your mind tonight. Listen, I can take you back home if you rather not help tonight."

"No. I want to help, I'm just thinking. Do you want kids?" Noah jerked his eyes to her, and then quickly turned back to the road. "I know that's a weird question and I don't mean with me, just in general. A general question."

"That's not a general question," Noah replied. "But yes, I would love to have kids one day. Two, three, twelve of them."

"Twelve?" Sammy squeaked out and Noah laughed.

"Ok, maybe three or four. What about you? Just, you know, generally."

"Yes," she said, without thinking. "I've always wanted three kids, but I'm also not getting any younger, so I may have to lower that number to two."

"Sammy, you aren't that old."

"I'm almost thirty-five. Don't tell me I'm not getting too old to have kids."

"I wasn't, but I know plenty of women who have kids in their thirties."

"Yeah, but how many women *start* in their thirties. I bet they all already have kids." Noah pulled to a stop in front of the warehouse, put the truck in park and turned toward her.

"I feel like I'm in lose-lose situation," he told her. "I'm not sure what you want me to say."

"I'm sorry. You're right. I shouldn't take out my insecurities on you." Noah reached over and touched her arm.

"Insecurities are fine to have. In fact, we all have them about something. I've struggled my whole adult life on if I would be a good enough pastor, a good enough son, a good enough human. Will I be enough for my future wife? For my kids? But I'm learning to let those thoughts go. Insecurities shouldn't control our lives. Why are we having this conversation anyhow?" Sammy shrugged. "Is it because your birthday is coming up? When *is* your birthday?"

"My birthday is in a couple of weeks, so maybe that's it." Noah watched her for a moment longer.

"I bet you'll have beautiful babies," he finally said. Sammy instantly felt her face heat up.

"Let's get inside before they start to wonder about us." Noah loved to see her blush, of course there was no way he was going to tell her that. He watched her get out of the truck and then followed suit. He wondered if she had talked to Brock about the same thing. *Brock.* He was beginning to feel it was time to get the other guy out of the picture, but he couldn't afford to think about a future with Sammy, until they talked about him leaving. After all, no one knew he had submitted an application but the church board. It wasn't a guaranteed position. Noah felt like he needed to know how Sammy felt, knowing he was leaving, before he could reveal that he might be staying. Suddenly, a conversation about babies seemed like the lesser of two evils.

Their time at the warehouse went by fast and before long, Noah was driving her back to her house. "Rose asked me to come to a Woman's Sewing Circle Thursday night," Sammy said, as he turned onto her street.

"Can you sew?"

"No," she laughed. "But Rose said they would teach me. I can't believe I see her all the time at the bank, but never really talked to her. Thanks for introducing us. I think we've going to be great friends."

"No trouble at all," he said. He pulled into her driveway and shut off the truck. Undoing his seat belt, he turned to face her. "Sammy, can we talk for a minute?"

"Sure, what is it?" Sammy unfastened and turned so she leaned up against the door.

"I like you," he began after a moment of silence, then he stopped. A few seconds ticked by, and Sammy just watched him. Suddenly he started again. "I really like you and the last thing I want to do is hurt you, but it's killing me knowing that you split your time between me and Brock, but I know I don't have any right to ask you to stop and as much as I want to see where this thing between us is going, I'm not sure what or where my future is and I'm not sure what to do." Noah stopped and took a deep breath.

"Wow, that was one major run on sentence," Sammy teased, trying to relieve some of the tense filling the cab of the truck, but he didn't return the smile.

"I'm not looking for a commitment," he continued. "At least not right now. It wouldn't be fair of me to ask, but I want you to be fully aware that, as of this moment-right now, I'm due in Alabama soon to help a buddy there out with a ministry he's trying to start up. After that, I'm not sure yet. I have some feelers out, some applications put in places, but I'm not sure what's going to happen." Sammy knew he was leaving, but hearing him say the words, knowing that he had made plans, made her heart hurt. "I don't know what to do." He shook his head like he was trying to clear it.

"I don't either," Sammy admitted.

Sammy sat in one of the chairs in By the Book, sipping coffee. She held a book in one hand, and even though she was staring at the words, her mind was caught up in the conversation she and Noah had had the night before. She jerked her eyes around as the bell over the door chimed. "Hey, hey, Sammy," Brock said as he walked in. "Hope I'm not interrupting." He flopped down on the chair next to her.

"Just dealing with the throngs of people browsing books," she responded. Brock looked around the empty store.

"Right. Anyway, I was wondering if you wanted to grab some supper with me tonight?" Sammy pressed her lips together and closed her book. Setting it aside, she uncrossed her legs and turned to fully face Brock.

"Brock, thank you for the invitation, and I have enjoyed getting to know you again, but I just don't think there's anything developing between us." She waited while he processed her words. He looked away briefly, before bringing his eyes back to hers.

"I was wondering when he would win outright."

"*He?*" she questioned, although she knew the answer.

"Pastor Noah. Honestly, I was wondering what was taking you so long. I'm not blind, Sammy, I see the way you look at him, and equally important, I notice the way *he* looks at you and how he looks at *me*." He gave a light laugh. "I'm amazed he hasn't tried to run me over with that banana truck of his."

"Noah would never try to do that," she defended.

"I know, I know," Brock said with a smile. "I was joking. Anyway," he said as he stood up. "I think you two make a power team. If I had to lose out to someone, I'm glad it was to him."

"You didn't lose," Sammy insisted. "We aren't exactly dating; I just don't think you and I will be able to rekindle what we had."

"No, I don't guess we will. I'm happy for you, though. I like the guy, I really do." He bent and gave her a kiss on the cheek. "But don't let him know I said that."

"I'm sure he would say the same thing," Sammy laughed.

"See you around, Sammy." He gave her another smile and then turned to leave. Sammy closed her eyes for a moment but opened them again when she heard him say hello to Lucy.

"Fancy seeing Brock in a bookstore," Lucy said, walking in with two coffee cups.

"I just told him I didn't think we should see each other." Lucy stopped and looked at her friend.

"And how did he take it? How did *you* take it?"

"He took it remarkably well."

"So does this mean you're totally serious about Noah?" Lucy sat down and handed one of the cups over. Sammy didn't answer right away, instead she took a tentative sip of her coffee to check the temperature. She let the liquid warm her throat as she tried to gather her thoughts.

"I'm not sure. Noah told me last night that he's due in Alabama in a few weeks to help out with a ministry there. After that, he didn't know where God would lead him." Sammy took another sip of coffee. "I'm not sure if

I'm ready for that heartache."

"Who says it would have to be a heartbreak? Who's to say he won't stay?" Sammy shook her head.

"No, I couldn't ask him to stay anymore then he would ask me to go. This is my home, Lucy. You're here, my friends, my business. My whole life. I'm not ready to give that up." Lucy reached out and squeezed Sammy's hand.

"Girlfriend, you wished life was a little more exciting, but I don't think this is what you had in mind, huh?"

"No," Sammy said with a weak laugh. "Next time I start complaining, remind me not too."

"Anyhow, how was working with Comfort in the Chaos yesterday?"

"It's amazing. You should go with us next week."

"I would like that," Lucy agreed. "Seems like you and Noah both have a servant's heart. Helping with the food ministry, visiting the retirement home."

"It takes more than that to make a relationship work."

"But it's a start."

Sammy ate lunch by herself at the bookstore. Lucy invited her out, but she wanted to have some quiet time to think. She was just finishing when her phone dinged.

Noah: Hey, Sammy. How are you?

Sammy: I'm doing good. Just eating lunch.

Noah: Sorry. Did I interrupt?

Sammy: No, I'm by myself. And pretty much done.

Noah: I know it's short notice, but we are going out tonight for Suzanna's birthday. I was wondering if you would like to join us?

Sammy: I don't want to intrude.

Noah: It's not intruding if I invite you.

Sammy didn't answer back right away. Spending time with Noah by himself was one thing, but spending time with him with his family was something completely different. It seemed like that would be taking their already strange relationship to a whole different level. Finally, her phone buzzed with Noah trying to Facetime her. Taking a deep breath and smoothing out her hair, she hit accept. "There'll be pizza and ice cream," he said by way of greeting.

"That's tempting, but I would still feel like an outsider."

"Why? Janet, Ken and the kids adore you. Suzanna would be so happy if you came, and so would her uncle." He flashed a real smile, dimples, and all.

"No fair throwing the kids in like that." *Or the dimples.*

"Hey, I'm just trying to turn the tide in my favor. Is it working? Don't make me beg?" He forced a frown and batted his eyelashes at the camera, causing Sammy to laugh. "Come on, sweetheart, say yes." Noah watched her over the phone. He hadn't meant to call her that. It had been a slip of the tongue, but the endearment was out now, and he wasn't going to apologize for it. At least, not right away. He figured he would watch her reaction, before saying anything else. He watched as she stopped laughing and her eyes got round with surprise. He waited.

"Ok," she finally said. "I'd love to come. What time?"

"I'll pick you up at 6:30. Is that okay?" She nodded and the bell above her door chimed.

"I'll let you go. See you tonight." Before she could form a goodbye, he disconnected the call.

"Welcome to By the Book," she was able to say, turning to welcome her customers.

Sammy and Noah pulled into a parking place at the Pizza Galaxy. "That really didn't happen," Sammy accused. "No way." She wiped at the tears rolling down her face from laughing.

"Totally serious. It was the funniest thing ever. Two grown men with mud covering their whole bodies, twigs and leaves stuck to the mud, one was missing a flip flop."

"I'm still not sure if I believe you or not," Sammy told him, as she unbuckled her seat belt and got out of the truck.

"Why would I lie?" He asked, coming around the truck to meet her. He noticed her gaze was fixed on something further down and turned to look. "What is it?"

"I'm fairly certain that's Brock down there. At least that's his car." He watched the scene unfold. At the other end of the strip mall was a pool hall, that often got a little rowdy. Brock was backed up against his car in the parking lot. From the streetlight that was close by, he could see three other men stood around him. He couldn't make out their words, but the tone carried on the wind.

"Stay here," he told Sammy.

"What are you going to do?" she asked, grabbing his hand as he started to turn away. He smiled at her.

"I'm going to do what I do best," he said. "Talk." He walked down the parking lot and causally called out. "Brock, my man, sorry we're late. You ready to grab that pizza?" Four sets of eyes turned to him, and he offered them a wide smile. He kept his hands out of his pockets so they could see he wasn't carrying a weapon.

"Um, yeah, Pastor, I'm starving." Brock tried to move from the car, but the biggest man glared at him, and he stopped.

"Look *Pastor*, this doesn't involve you. I suggest that you head on back where you came from," the biggest man spat. Noah clicked his tongue in disagreement.

"I'm afraid I can't do that. You see, Brock goes to my church, so I feel like I'm obligated to help him out no matter what dumb thing he's done. I mean, what *did* he do this time?"

"Well, your boy here tried playing us for a fool. Now he needs to be taught a lesson. We don't look kindly on a pool shark." Noah scowled over at Brock who just shrugged.

"You and I are having a serious talk later." Then looking back at the group. "Look, I don't really need to know the details, but I'm afraid I can't leave without him." One of the other men stepped toward Noah. He was bigger than Noah, and Noah had to tilt his chin up to look the other guy in the eye. The man cracked his knuckles and sneered.

"Look, Preacher man," he said. "If you know what's good for you, you'll turn around and get lost." Noah shook his head. The other guy threw a fast punch toward Noah, who surprised everybody by catching the fist in his own hand and stopping its motion. For a moment, they simply stared at each other.

"I'm not going to fight you," Noah said. "And I'm not going to let you beat the idiot up either." All four of the men- Brock included, looked at him in shock. Noah pushed the hand away from him, and dug his feet into the ground, preparing for the next blow, but it never came.

"Come on, boys, these two jerks aren't worth our time anymore." He glared at Brock and then at Noah, but the three left without another incident. Once they were all back inside the pool hall, Noah turned his eyes to Brock.

"You *are* an idiot," he said. "Come on. Let's go grab pizza." He turned and began to walk away.

"Pastor." Noah glanced back over his shoulder. "Thanks."

Noah was glad that Janet didn't mind one more person at the party, even if he felt a little odd about Brock being there. He also found it odd that he wasn't on their end of the table, trying to tell Sammy his side of the story. Instead, he had opted to sit down beside one of Janet's single friends. "Penny for your thoughts." Noah looked over at Sammy. When she smiled questioningly at him, he realized that he had missed something she was saying.

"I'm sorry, what?"

"I said thank you."

"For what?" Noah wondered how much of the conversation he had tuned out. Sammy laughed at the confused look on his face.

"For rescuing Brock," she repeated. "Who knows what those guys would have done to him if you hadn't shown up."

"I didn't intercede on his behalf," he clarified. Sammy leaned over and gave him a kiss on the cheek. It was quick and gentle, and Noah wondered if he had imagined it. "What was that for?"

"For being you. For stepping into a situation that you didn't have to. For interceding on my behalf. For being mad at Brock for flirting with another woman in front of me." Noah felt his cheeks begin to burn. "But you can stop drilling holes in his head with your eyes. I told Brock earlier today that I thought it was best if we didn't see each other anymore. Well, not *not* see each other, but, you know, go out. On dates. Together." Noah stared at her while he processed the statement. He wanted to ask why she had done that? What did it mean for him? For them? He had a million questions, but he just smiled at her, and when she returned it, his heart skipped a beat.

"Thank you for another wonderful and very eventful night." Sammy said to Noah as they climbed the steps to her front door. "Things are never dull when you're around."

"Maybe not the best qualification to put on my resume. Aren't pastors supposed to be dull and boring?"

He replied as she turned to face him. Sammy gave him a playful shove on the chest.

"No, they are not. And you, Noah, are unquestionably to most undull, unboring guy I think I've ever met."

"Oh?" He raised a questioning eyebrow. "Not simply an undull, unboring pastor?" Sammy shook her head.

"Nope, I'm fairly certain I've never met another guy as- *interesting* as you."

"Why, Miss Felton, I do believe that's the nicest thing you've ever said to me," he teased, reaching out and tucking a piece of stray hair behind her ear. Sammy felt heat creeping up her neck, and her throat went dry. His hand lingered briefly before he slid the back of his fingers over her jaw line. It was all she could do not to close her eyes and lean into the touch. He cupped her face and searched her eyes. Slowly, he leaned toward her, until his mouth almost touched hers. He whispered her name. Asking permission to proceed. Giving her time to back away, but she closed the distance between their lips. It was a feather light touch at first. Then his lips began to move against hers. One hand slid into her hair, and his other wrapped around her waist to pull her closer. Sammy reached up and fisted the front of his shirt, using him to hold herself up. Her heart began to race the moment their lips met, and the ground fell away when he deepened the kiss.

"Wow," she whispered once the kiss ended. His mouth still hovered close to hers, and she could feel his heart racing under her hand. He touched his forehead to hers and smiled.

"Wow," he repeated.

"You can say that again." A third voice made them jump away from each other, and when Lucy started to clap, both their faces turned red. "I mean it, wow. That was a performance and a half. Well done, Pastor, and honestly, it's about time." Sammy shot her friend a death glare and gave Noah a look of embarrassment.

"Sorry," she mouthed to Noah, but he just smiled and took it in stride.

"Goodbye, Lucy," he said in a stern voice. She stuck out her lip in a pout but turned and went back inside, leaving the door open. "Good night, Samantha." He leaned forward and gave her a gentle kiss on the lips, before leaving.

"I can't believe you," Sammy started the moment she shut the front door. Lucy sat on the arm of the couch; a grin plastered on her face. "Of all the times you decide to interrupt."

"I honestly didn't mean to. I heard his truck pull up and wanted to see if the rumor mill was right. But I must say, finding you and Noah steaming up the front steps was a bonus I'll take even if you are going to tie all my bras in a knot."

"What rumor?" Sammy questioned.

"Did he get in a fight tonight?" Sammy covered her face and flopped into a chair with a groan.

"How? How did you already hear about that?"

"Wait, so Jenny was right? Noah was in a fight?" She fell backwards off the arm and landed on her back. "I don't believe it."

"He wasn't *in* a fight, but he did break one up. He pretty much saved Brock from getting beat up by three guys. And then he invited him to join us for dinner."

"He did *what?*" Sammy told her all about how Noah stopped the fight, and Brock having dinner with them and how Noah had gone all jealous. She even told her about their conversation leading up to the kiss on the front porch. "Well, no wonder the boy finally kissed you."

"What do you mean?" Sammy questioned. Sitting up, Lucy crossed her legs and leaned forward.

"All this time you have referred to him as a pastor, or at least that's how I've heard you always refer to him. And tonight, you called him a guy. An undull, unboring guy. You're finally seeing him first as a *man* and not just a pastor." Sammy opened her mouth to object but closed it with a snap. Was Lucy right? She tried to think back to all their past conversations. Had she always referred to him as a pastor or a preacher? Suddenly her head began to throb, and her energy disappeared.

"I'm going to bed. Good night, Lucy."

Noah was in his room the next day, when Janet threw open the door, and glared at him. "You!" She marched in and stopped inches from him. "You didn't tell me the whole story about last night. You said you ran into Brock in the parking lot. You left out the part about the three thugs you had an altercation with."

"Janet, does it look like I was in a fight?" He indicated his face and held up his hands. "Not a bruise or cut."

"Then why am I getting phone calls?"

"Because this town is full of nosy busy bodies with nothing else to do then make my life hard," he answered, pushing past his sister.

"While that's true, I think you owe me an answer."

"The answer is simple. Brock got himself into a tight spot, as a pastor, I stepped in to defuse the situation. There was one punch thrown by one of the other guys. I stopped it. They walked away. I invited Brock to join us because I felt better being able to see him. End of story. I have no idea why it's all over the town. I didn't fight. I didn't throw a punch. Promise." Janet watched her brother for a moment, before letting her anger go.

"I'm sorry I jumped to the wrong conclusion. I just worry about you."

"I know you do, Sis, but I'm a big boy now. I can take care of myself."

"Yes, I know. And I also know as a black belt in material arts, your hands can be considered a deadly weapon." Noah walked to her and put his hands on her shoulders.

"I'm not going to do anything to jeopardize my job or my reputation, or yours for that matter."

"Speaking of job. I also heard a whisper through the rumor mill that Pastor Gene asked you to consider applying to be our full time Worship Pastor."

"What is with this town? You haven't said anything to anybody, have you?" Janet shook her head.

"So, it's true. Why haven't you said anything?" Noah walked over to his bed and sat down.

"I don't know. Yes, I do. Because of Sammy. I like her more than I want to admit, but by leaving, knowing I'm leaving, it keeps a wall between us."

"Noah, that makes no sense whatsoever. If you like her, shouldn't you be looking for ways to stay?"

"I'm scared. I've spent so many years punishing myself for my past mistakes, convincing myself that I didn't deserve to be happy, that I'm not sure what to do with all these…feelings." Janet sat down and hugged him.

"Baby Brother, I want you to be happy. God wants you to be happy. Instead of thinking about the places you think God is leading you, have you thought about that He led you here? That He put Sammy in your path for a reason? You two have so much in common. Maybe you need to figure out who is telling you to leave- God or you?" She gave him another squeeze and then left him to his own thoughts. He felt bad for not telling Janet that he had already applied for the position, but he needed everybody to believe that he was leaving. At least until his sermon. He grabbed his phone and pushed himself up the bed, until his back was against the headboard.

Noah: Did you hear about the first restaurant to open on the moon?

Sammy: Great. We're back to the jokes. No, I haven't heard about it.

Noah: It had good food, but no atmosphere

Sammy: *eye roll* Booooo

Noah: I have a ton of them, sweetheart.

Sammy: That's what I'm afraid of.

Noah: What are you doing tonight?

Sammy: Ummm, I don't know. Let me think. Oh, yes, going to church.

Noah: To sound like a 7th grade kid, do you want to sit with me during dinner?

Sammy: lol. That does sound very middle school-ish.

Noah: I'll even carry your books.

Sammy: Better watch out. People may start talking.

Noah: I'm already known as the Fighting Pastor. So, I say let them talk. I'll see you tonight.

Sammy smiled at her phone. "Tell Noah hello for me," Lucy teased. She sat in one of the chairs in the bookstore. Sammy quickly slid her phone into her pocket. "I guessed that right, didn't I."

"Yes, you did. We were making plans to sit together tonight at dinner." Lucy gave a low whistle.

"Well, well, well," she said with a smile. "Things are moving right along, aren't they?"

"That's the problem." Sammy came around the counter and sat in one of the free chairs. "What happens when he leaves?"

"Why does it feel like we've had the conversation before? Oh, yes, because we have." Lucy took a sip of her coffee. "Look, Sammy, we don't live in the dark ages. We have cell phones. And video calls. And these things called cars that can drive us to people we love."

"Love?" Sammy repeated. "Hold up, nobody has mentioned the 'l' word."

"Maybe not, but that doesn't mean others don't see it." Before Sammy could respond, the door opened, and

Esther walked in.

"Good morning, Ms. Esther," Sammy and Lucy said together and then began to laugh.

"Good morning, you two. Sammy, dear, just the lady I wanted to see." Lucy looked down at her watch.

"Oh, my goodness, I'm late. I'll see you both tonight." She grabbed her purse and hurried out the door.

"I hope she didn't leave on my account," Esther said, walking over to the counter.

"Oh, no. She's got to be to work in about three minutes." Sammy laughed and motioned toward the seat Lucy had just abandoned. "Can I get you some coffee?"

"No, thank you, love. I just popped in to pick up that book that I ordered."

"Of course. Let me go grab it from the back room." Esther was browsing a small rack of clearance books when Sammy returned. "Do you want me to go ahead and ring this up, or are you still looking?"

"Go ahead. One new book is good enough for now." She put back the book she was looking at and walked to the counter. "So how are things with Young Noah going?" Sammy kept her eyes on the computer screen.

"Um, it's going ok." She wasn't sure how to answer that question. They had been out a few times- both as friends and on dates. *How were things supposed to be going?*

"That's so wonderful to hear. He's such a nice young man." Sammy nodded but didn't answer.

"That'll be twelve dollars and twenty-four cents." Esther handed over a twenty-dollar bill.

"I don't suppose I ever told you about when Gene and I started dating. Oh, my goodness, that was way back in the dawn of time." Sammy smiled and handed over the change. "Thank you." She dropped the money in her purse and took the bag Sammy held out. "I was just seventeen when we met, and Gene was nineteen and working at a car garage. My parents came unglued. Here I was, an innocent young lady with a line of suitable bachelors to choose from, back then girls got married young- there wasn't a lot of careers for us to go into, and the man who had caught my eye was this tall young hellion with jet black hair and a cigarette hanging out of his mouth. Oh, and a motorcycle." She giggled as she remembered her past.

"I bet he was a sight to see," Sammy agreed, leaning on the counter to listen.

"Yes, he was. Of course, we didn't start dating right away, my father forbade it, but we would sneak off and met down by the creek near this one particular tree. Oddly enough, Noah's brother-in-law's family owns the land now." Sammy's hear skipped a beat. The tree by the creek where Noah had first pressed a kiss to her hand, with the heart and the initials. "We would talk for hours- about everything and nothing at all. About six months before my eighteenth birthday, my parents sent me to my great-aunt's house up in Virginia. They thought the distance would make me forget about Gene and all the crazy ideas I had about marring him."

"This is sounding like a book. Have you ever thought about writing it?" Esther waved a hand dismissively.

"Oh, goodness no. Who would want to read this

sappy old story?"

"What happened next? Obviously, you and Pastor meet back up and got married, so your father's plan didn't work."

"I wrote that boy letters almost every day I was away. My cousin would take them to town and mail them for me. And when he wrote back, she would intercept them before my Aunt could get them. The moment I turned eighteen, I kissed them both goodbye and high tailed it back. Gene was waiting for me with flowers and a ring. I'm not going to say it's been easy. He had a well-deserved reputation that followed him for years. But we stuck it out, through jail time, through his drinking, through kids. I can't imagine my life without him. God truly has grown us together."

"What an amazing story," Sammy said, elbow propped on the counter with her chin resting in her hand. "Why can't we all have something like that?" Esther reached out and patted Sammy's free hand.

"Most of us can if we don't overlook what's in front of us. See you tonight, dear." With that the older lady left the store, and left Sammy alone with her thoughts.

Chapter 13

"Gotten into any more fights, Pastor?" Brock teased Noah as they made their way down the food line.

"Not yet, but the night is still young," Noah answered back with a laugh. Sammy shook her head.

"I don't know how you two can joke about what happened. Those guys were huge. You both could have been injured."

"But we weren't," Noah said. "God had my back."

"And Pastor had mine," Brock threw in.

"Talk to you later, Brock," Noah tossed over his shoulder as they gathered napkins and grabbed drinks.

"You two seem to be cozy," Sammy commented as they made their way to a back table.

"We had a nice long talk today."

"Really? As in buddy to buddy or man to pastor?" Noah gave her his lopsided grin but didn't answer her question.

"How was your day?" he asked instead.

"That's what I thought." Sammy held out her hand and when Noah took it, she offered a quick grace before they began to eat. "And my day was good, thank you for asking. So other than fulfilling your pastoral duties, what have you been up to?"

"I'm afraid not much too exciting. Talked to Gary about going out with the dinner crew on Saturday night since they are short a few people. Then talked to my buddy over in Alabama about when I'll be there to help him." He ate several bites of his food, before continuing. "I, umm, took a phone call from a pastor out in Wyoming."

"Wyoming? Another friend of yours?" Sammy questioned.

"Not exactly," he answered. "The pastor at my old church, he, umm, gave this guy my number. They're looking for an Assistant Pastor for their church and wants me to apply." Sammy stopped with her fork halfway to her mouth.

"Wow, that's…that's great news, right? You've been wondering where God would lead you, and this could be a big step." Noah pushed the food around his plate, his eyes firmly fixed on his beans rolling around.

"Yeah… yeah, it could be." They were both quiet for a few minutes before Noah finally lifted his eyes. "Samantha." Sammy looked up at him and waited for him to continue. When he didn't, she simply reached over and took his hand.

"I know," she said, understanding the unknowing that hung in the air.

Noah was happy that Sammy decided to sit closer to the front. After his three songs, Pastor Gene came onto stage, and Noah retreated the few pews to where Sammy sat. He smiled as he sat down beside her but felt the heat creep up his neck when he noticed a few people cast knowing looks their way. "I thought you didn't care if people talked," Sammy whispered out the corner of her mouth.

"I don't," he whispered back. "But that doesn't mean that I like being the center of their attention." Sammy pinched her lips together to keep from laughing but reached over and took his hand. It was a bold move considering they weren't officially dating. Were they? *Then why are we talking about future plans?* They sat, holding hands, and listening to Gene's sermon. Noah was reluctant to let go when Gene called him back to the stage for one last song. He gave her fingers a squeeze and made his way forward.

"While I've got Pastor Noah coming back to sing, I want to remind everybody that a week from Sunday will be his last day as our Temporary Worship Pastor for us." A murmur went through the room, but Noah couldn't decide if it was happy or sad. He gave Gene a forced smile, as the older man put an arm around his shoulders. "Pastor Noah doesn't know this, but we will be having a dinner that day after service." Noah's heart tightened with gratitude. "I hope that you'll plan on joining us as we help the good Pastor celebrate his next assignment. And one more thing, this coming Sunday, Noah has requested a chance to preach one more sermon to you." Gene patted him on the back, then motioned for him to take the stage to sing.

Noah barely made it through the closing song. He barely made it through shaking hands, and the small talk that came after service. *Two more Sundays.* That was it. He had two more Sundays to decide his future. Because if the church didn't hire him, then what? He knew he had to listen to what God was telling him. The problem was, he didn't know what God was saying. Everything was confused in his mind, in his heart. On the one hand he prayed that the church offered him a job. He would be doing what he loved, close to his family, and close to Sammy. On the other hand, was he letting his earthly wants get in the way of his spiritual duties? By the time Noah made it out of the sanctuary, he was mentally and spiritually drained. He looked for Sammy but didn't see her in the hallway or the fellowship hall. She wasn't in any of the Sunday School rooms or his office. He pushed through the front doors of the church and his heart skipped a beat as he approached his truck and noticed his tail gate was down and Sammy was sitting waiting for him. "I was wondering where you disappeared to," he said, taking a seat beside her.

"I figured you would be busy for a while. Everybody seemed to want to talk to you."

"How about you? Do you want to talk too?" Sammy stared off into the distance.

"I just wanted to see if you wanted to do dinner tomorrow night?" She turned her head to find him watching her. He searched her eyes, her face, her soul for a moment.

"I'll like that."

"Good. Why don't you come by the house at seven-thirty? I'd like to cook supper for you. Lucy will be there, so it'll be all proper and everything. I'll just banish her to her room with popcorn and a movie. Maybe some Twizzlers if I'm feeling gracious."

"Sounds perfect." Sammy hopped up off the tail

gate, and Noah followed.

"Great. See you then."

"Samantha." His voice stopped her, and she slowly turned back to him. Noah took a step forward and dropped a gentle kiss on her lips. "See you tomorrow." She smiled, and then turned and walked off to her car. With a deep sigh, Noah got into his truck and headed back to Janet's and to the solitude of his room to pray.

"You can't cook and clean at the same time, can you?" Lucy looked around the kitchen and tsked her tongue. "It's a war zone in here."

"I know," Sammy agreed. "I'm about to start cleaning. I still have time before Noah gets here. What?" She questioned when Lucy leaned back against the counter and smiled.

"I just like watching you get flustered."

"That's not nice."

"I know." Pushing herself away from the counter, Lucy began to pick up dirty bowls and pots.

"You don't have to do that," Sammy protested.

"I know that too, but that's what friends do." Lucy started to rinse the dishes and put them into the dishwasher. "So have you and Noah talked about what happens when he leaves?" Sammy slammed down the pot she was moving from the stove to the counter.

"Sorry," she apologized. "Not in so many words. I know he's leaving. I know he's got a job offer in Wyoming."

"Wyoming, wow. That's more than a day trip away,

huh?"

"I know, which means I am still as confused as ever. I mean, we aren't even officially dating. Are we? How do you even know if you're exclusive?" Lucy shrugged as she gathered dishes.

"In high school your boyfriend would give you his class ring to show that you were going steady, but I think that's called getting engaged at our age."

"Which we are not going to be doing," Sammy interrupted. "It's only been a few weeks."

"Of course," Lucy agreed. "So, umm, I don't know. I guess you know you're *exclusive* when you just don't go out with anybody else."

"Big help you are."

"Sorry, it's all I've got. I'm not a relationship expert," Lucy laughed. They had just finished cleaning the kitchen when the front doorbell rang. "That's either my pizza or your beau. I'll check." Before Sammy could protest, Lucy skipped- *yes, skipped*- out of the kitchen. A quick check through the peephole confirmed it was Noah, and she threw the door open.

"Your pizza, madam," Noah said with a cheesy smile and holding out a pizza box.

"Now how did you get my pizza?" Lucy questioned, taking the box and ushering him inside.

"I'm a man of many secrets. That and the pizza guy pulled in behind me. Thought I would save him the trip." Lucy laughed and closed the door.

"As long as I get my pizza, I don't really care who brings it to the door. Sammy, Noah is here, and he's come with gifts." She eyed the bag in his hand. Lucy gave him a grin before turning to Sammy as she walked into the living room. "I'm just going to take my pizza and soda and head upstairs to binge watch my favorite show. You kids have fun." Sammy rolled her eyes as Lucy left the room.

"She can join us," Noah said. "I really don't mind."

"Are you crazy? She wouldn't turn down pizza and TV for Shephard's pie and conversation." Noah closed the distance between them, and Sammy wrapped him in a hug. Drawing back slightly, Noah dropped a kiss to her mouth.

"I've been waiting for that since the last one," he told her.

"It's hasn't been that long."

"Long enough."

"Come on through. Dinner is almost ready." Noah followed her into the kitchen, where she had sat the table with plates and silverware.

"It smells wonderful. Oh, this is for you." Sammy looked at the bag he held out.

"You didn't have to bring me anything.

"I know, and it's not much, but I thought you would like it. Take it." Giving him a smile, she took the bag and peaked inside.

"Oh, Noah, I love it." Reaching in, she pulled out a shirt with *Comfort in the Chaos Ministries* across the front along with their logo.

"Now when we go out, we'll match the rest of the volunteers. That is, if you still want to go."

169

"Of course," she quickly answered.

"But?" He said, encouraging her to continue. She looked at the shirt and then back at him.

"But," she began slowly, "if you've forgotten, you're leaving in just over a week. And I'm not sure I want to continue serving without you. I mean, you're the whole reason I found out about them, anyhow." Noah took a few steps toward her and took her hands.

"It doesn't matter if I'm here or not, you enjoy helping them out. You should keep doing it." Sammy nodded her agreement, too afraid to speak in case her voice betrayed her emotions. "Sammy." He reached up and cupped her cheek. "Look at me." She took a deep breath before lifting her eyes to his. "Talk to me." Dropping her eyes again, she shook her head and took a step back.

"Let's eat," she said instead. She heard him give a sigh, but he didn't say anything else as he followed her to the table.

Conversation flowed easily over dinner and dessert. "You're an amazing cook," Noah told her as they made their way into the living room, each with tall glasses of sweet tea.

"It was just Shepard's Pie. It's really hard to mess it up."

"And what about the chocolate lava cake? That was amazing." Sammy blushed. Sitting down on the couch, she tucked her legs under her, and turned to face him.

"So, tell me more about this job offer in Wyoming." Noah took a long drink and swallowed hard.

"Well," he began, placing his cup on the coffee table and leaning back. "It's in Wyoming."

"I know that silly."

"Not much else to tell. I would be Associate Pastor and Worship Leader. Basically, what I'm doing now, just a fancier title."

"Wouldn't that mean preaching more sermons? How do you feel about that?" Noah licked his lips. He turned to look more fully at her.

"I mean, I think I'm okay with it. Sammy, look, I haven't made up my mind if that's where I'm going yet. I've been praying nonstop. I think God may be laying something else on my heart."

"Noah, I've enjoyed our time together, but you can't make this choice based on me, or us and a budding relationship. You need to do what's best for you."

"Doesn't mean that you don't play a part in it, though. Don't worry," he said as she opened her mouth to protest. "I'm not going to overrule God."

"Good."

"But there is something that I need to tell you." Sammy waited patiently as Noah gathered his thoughts. "I need you to promise not to tell anybody." When she nodded her understanding, he went on. "I, um, I've applied for another job. The permanent Worship Pastor job here but there is one small problem." Sammy bit her lip to keep from squealing.

"Noah, that's- I don't know what to say. You didn't apply just because of me, did you?"

"I can't deny that I care for you. And yes, you were

part of my choice, but it would also mean I would be close to Janet and the kids."

"But what about Alabama?"

"Ah, yes, well, I still have to head there, but it would only be for a few weeks."

"Wait, you said there was a problem. It certainly not because the Pastor doesn't like you." Noah smiled.

"No, it's not Pastor Gene. This sermon I'm preaching on Sunday. It's my testimony. I'm coming clean about my drug use, and my part in someone dying and my jail time. Everything. The board may interview me, but it's the church members that have to agree to offer me a job."

"Oh, Noah," she said, sliding over to him. "Everybody at church thinks you're wonderful, I can't image them not offering it to you."

"I hope you're right, Sammy." She smiled. Then leaned over and gave him a kiss.

Chapter 14

"Are you ready?" Sammy asked, as she stood in Noah's office and watched him pace back and forth.

"No," he answered with a shake of his head. "Sammy, what if this is a terrible idea? What if this blows any chance that they'll offer me the job? What if...?"

"What if you go out there and rock it? You've got to do this. This is who you are, it's part of you. And if they decide not to offer you the job, then this just isn't where you're supposed to be." At those words, Noah stopped and looked at her. His blue eyes were almost gray with worry.

"But what if this is where I want to be?"

"Don't overrule God, remember?"

"And I'm not trying to," Noah said, walking over to where she stood. "I'm just...I'm not ready to go." Sammy smiled and reached up and placed a hand on his cheek.

"Do your best out there," she told him. "Remember, they all love you." Noah reached up and covered her hand with his.

"And what about you?" The sound of the clock ticking was the only sound between them. Neither dared to move until a tap came at the partially closed door. Sammy dropped her hand but didn't step away and didn't break eye contact.

"Sorry to interrupt," Pastor Gene said, pushing the door open and smiling at the two of them.

"No worries," Noah answered, turning to look at the older man. "What can I help you with?"

"I just came to check on you. See how things are going. How are you feeling?"

"Nervous, scared out of my mind." Noah said honestly. "Beginning to think this was the worst idea I've ever had."

"All those things are normal, Noah, and again, you don't have to do this." Noah was already shaking his head before the other man finished.

"No, everybody out there has the right to know me and my past before they vote on keeping me or not." Gene nodded his understanding.

"Noah, son, you are a good man and a good pastor. I'm sure Sammy has already told you this, but every person out there thinks the world of you already." Noah glanced over at Sammy at the words, then took a deep breath. "Come on, you two, lets pray before we head out."

Noah led a beautiful selection of songs, before he put his guitar down and walked down the steps to stand in front of the stage. He let his eyes drift over the faces before him and thought of all the new friends he had made in his time at this church. He saw Gene and Esther sitting in the front pew. Janet, Ken and Sammy were together just a few pews back. So many memories were already flooding through his mind. "I want to start by saying, thank you. Thank you for giving me the chance to come here and lead the singing and the chances you've given me to preach. When Janet contacted me about coming here, I'll admit I didn't really want to come. Nothing against any of you, but a small-town church was not on my radar." He took another deep breath.

"I know Pastor Gene introduced me that first night here, but I would like to take the time to let you get to know me a little better. The first thing you need to know about me, Noah Sinclair, is that I didn't grow up in the best home." He saw Ken slide an arm around Janet's shoulders. "I'm not going to go into many details, but it's important that you know that there was abuse and drinking and just not happy times. I'm telling you that, so you understand the next part on the story." He nodded to the man in the sound booth and a picture popped up on the overhead screen. A soft murmur went through the room. "Yup, that's me," he continued. "Wild and free." The picture showed a younger Noah standing in a garage in ripped jeans and a black muscle shirt. He was playing the guitar and his hair was flying around his head. "You can tell a lot from pictures but what you can't tell is that behind that mane of shaggy hair was a fifteen-year-old drug addict." Another murmur went through the room and Noah waited for it to settle. "You see, Janet and our other sister turned to books and school and friends to help cope with our homelife. Me- I turned to music and then to drugs." Noah moved from one side of the stage to the other. He made sure he talked to the whole audience. "Let's fast forward a bit. I apologize in advance for this next picture." On the screen, a picture of Noah standing in front of a college flashed up. The same shaggy hair and ripped jeans. His jean jacket was dirty and covered in patches and he was flipping dual birds at the camera. "I blurred my hands, but I think you can all guess what's behind those blurry dots." Heads bobbed up and down.

"If you weren't amazed that I made it through high school while addicted to drugs, then how about the fact I graduated with good enough grades to get into college. This was my first day. My mom was so happy for me. Her and my sisters helped move me in, kissed me goodbye and I turned right around and got high." He was moving again. "Things went okay for most of that year. I held my own, made decent grades. Then, *it* happened." He stopped and his eyes caught Sammy's- who nodded. "The single event that changed the course of my life forever. I was at a party, and I pushed a friend to try some stuff that had been pulled out. Even though he didn't want to, he finally gave into me and the rest of the guys. He ended up having an allergic reaction and died a few days later." At that people started talking and Noah waited.

"Anyhow, the next few months were a wreck. I dealt with things the only way I knew, and that way landed me in jail." On the screen a mug shot of a 19-year-old Noah flashed. Face bruised and bloody from a fight. A shocked gasped sounded. "It was while there that I met Pastor Buck Kingston." A picture came on of Noah with his arm around an older gentleman with soft brown eyes and tattoos. "That guy right there saved my life. He showed up when I didn't want him to. He talked when I didn't want to listen. He wouldn't go away even when I told him where to go. Even offered to draw him a map. And because he stayed true to his calling, I found mine. He's the reason I listened when God spoke. He's the reason that I became a pastor." Noah paused for a moment as people whispered between them.

"I have always thought I had to hide my past. I felt

that if I let people know me, know where I came from then you would see me as a fake." He shook his head. "Even though my heart knew God had forgiven me, my mind wouldn't fully believe it. It took coming here for that to change. It took Janet inviting me here and giving me a place to stay. And her family- *my* family- accepting me as one of their own." The people laughed when a picture of Noah on the floor with Suzanna and Jude sitting on him and Janet tickling his feet. "It took Pastor Gene to tell me that I was here for a reason and to reiterate what Brother Buck had been telling me for years." A picture of Noah and Gene sitting at a kitchen table came up. "It took Brock to remind me that being a pastor means stepping in when you might would rather step away." Everybody laughed at the picture that came up. Noah and Brock facing each other, both in fighting stances.

"I've got your back, brother," Brock called from the back of the sanctuary, sending another round of laughter.

"And it took a very special friend to help teach me that being a man of God meant letting go of my shame and living how He sees me." When the picture of him and Sammy sitting on his tailgate came up, the sound of aww filled his ears. "Samantha, you convinced me that it was okay to forgive myself. That I didn't need to live in this self-imposed prison that I had sentenced myself to. God had already forgiven me, that it was time to forgive myself." Noah looked out over the crowd. He took in every face that was becoming family to him. He saw Janet and Sammy holding hands, both smiling at him. He saw Gene nodding his head in approval. He saw his future out in the pews. "I'm a recovering drug addict. A man with a messed-up background. A sinner with a history.

A preacher with a story that I hope can help touch other people. I'm not sure where my future lays." He took a deep breath. "But I pray that I'll always have the courage to be open about who I am and what brought me to this point." He called Pastor Gene up to offer the closing prayer, and while eyes were closed, Noah quietly slipped out of the sanctuary, down the hall and out the back door of the church. He needed to escape the confines of the walls and the voices of the people. He quickly made his way across the backlot of the church to a small pond that sat just beyond the trees. He had asked Gene about the area not long after arriving and was told it was church property, but other than cutting the grass, it was mainly unmanaged. He found his favorite spot under a shady live oak tree and sat. The bark was rough through his shirt, and the ground soft with early spring grass. He let his head fall back against the tree and closed his eyes to the world.

"That was some testimony you delivered, Pastor," Sammy said as she approached, and took a sit beside him, her shoulder touching his.

"Then like a coward, I ran away." Noah kept his eyes closed.

"No one thinks you're a coward," she told him. "In fact, everyone had only positive things to say, as far as I heard. Pastor Gene said, once he was finished and you were gone, that sometimes, when we lay ourselves wide open for people, empty ourselves, God calls us away so that He can refill our soul. I think everybody understands that you needed a moment to yourself." Sammy felt him take a deep breath.

"I think," he began, "I think that was the single

hardest thing I've ever done."

"And you did it brilliantly."

"You know, I do feel lighter. I thought telling you about my past lifted a burden, but as I spoke to the whole church, I don't know." He shook his head. "It was like I felt something lifting from me. Like I finally released everything holding me back."

"I know that your future is still uncertain," Sammy started as she reached over and interlaced their fingers. "But I want you to know that I'm part of it, no matter what. No matter where." Noah quickly opened his eyes as he turned to look at her.

"Sammy, I can't ask you to leave."

"You didn't," she countered. "But you asked me a question earlier today. The answer is that I love you, Noah, and I'm willingly going wherever you go." She watched his eyes brighten and a smile spread across his face.

"I love you too, Samantha," he said, before leaning over and giving her a kiss.

Epilogue

7 months later

Noah held the door to his newly redecorated office open for Sammy. "It's beautiful," she said. The whole room was done in gray, white, sand and accents of bright cyan. "It's like being at the beach."

"That's what we were hoping for," he answered. On one wall hung a large canvas with "Don't Overrule God" wrote on it and pictures of beach scenes.

"I'm sorry it took so long to get a proper office."

"Between my time in Alabama, and my probation period here, I understand why they made me wait. Worth it, though." Sammy offered him a smile, as she continued to wander the room. "How's the Comfort in the Chaos Closet coming along?"

"Almost ready to open. Just a few more things to iron out." She stopped at his desk and laughed when she saw the picture of them on the tailgate. "Do you really have to have this in here?" she questioned.

"I love that picture," Noah said.

"Not sure why."

"Because," he started as he wrapped his arms around her. "That's the moment I knew that I loved you."

"You're just saying that." Noah offered her his lopsided smile.

"Believe what you want," he said, dropping a kiss on her lips.

"Are we still on for tonight? Gary said he really needed help because three people have the flu."

"Wouldn't miss it," he answered, as he let her pull away from him and start toward the door. "You know," he said. "I might be willing to replace the selfie picture."

"With a new selfie?" Sammy threw back over her shoulder.

"How about with our wedding picture?" Sammy swung around to find Noah on one knee and a diamond ring held up toward her. A gasped escaped before her hands came up to cover her mouth. "Samantha, I love you more than I ever thought was possible. I know that God led me here just so I could find you, and there is no one else I want to spend the rest of my days with. I promise to be the best husband, father, man I can be. Will you marry me?"

"Oh, Noah." Sammy was already nodding as she took a few steps that separated them and dropped to her knees in front of him. "Absolutely, yes." Noah slipped the ring on her finger and then gathered her in his arms and sealed his promise with a kiss.